SEX & SUBMISSION

A collection of twenty erotic stories

Edited by Cathryn Cooper

Published by Accent Press Ltd – 2007
ISBN 1905170793 / 9781905170791

Printed and bound in the UK by
Creative Design and Print

Cover Design by
Red Dot Design

Publication 14th February 2007

Sex & Seduction	**1905170785**	**price £7.99**
Sex & Satisfaction	**1905170777**	**price £7.99**
Sex & Submission	**1905170793**	**price £7.99**

Publication 14th May 2007

5 Minute Fantasies 1	**1905170610**	**price £7.99**
5 Minute Fantasies 2	**190517070X**	**price £7.99**
5 Minute Fantasies 3	**1905170718**	**price £7.99**

Publication 13th August 2007

Whip Me	**1905170920**	**price £7.99**
Spank Me	**1905170939**	**price £7.99**
Tie Me Up	**1905170947**	**price £7.99**

Publication 12th November 2007

Ultimate Sins	**1905170599**	**price £7.99**
Ultimate Sex	**1905170955**	**price £7.99**
Ultimate Submission	**1905170963**	**price £7.99**

Contents

Darkness
by January James

I used to be afraid of the dark, until you showed me just how wonderful it could be. Losing my sight behind a blindfold has over time sharpened my other senses dramatically. As soon as you cover my eyes I become a different person. I can smell the paraffin wax candles, the sounds of your heavy breathing, even though you have yet to descend the basement stairs. I can smell your cock, the glistening, sweaty sweetness of your body.

I know that you're watching me. I stand a little taller. I can feel the worship in your eyes. Though I'm bound like a slave I still feel like a queen.

I sense your eyes on my naked breasts, especially those areas that seem to be painted in the darker chocolate hue that accentuates my areolas. You love to try and get your mouth around it all. From there your eyes travel down my voluptuous chocolate body, over my flat stomach with the butterfly tattoo, to the kinky blackness of my sex; and further on to my softly sculpted things and long legs.

I have been waiting for hours. You woke me this morning by sticking your tongue between my legs, licking my body awake until every nerve was on fire.

Just when I thought that you would shove your morning hard-on into me you told me that you wanted to play this game. I love our games but I'm tired of waiting. I'm hungry in every way possible. I want to eat you, to feel the strength of your hardness under my tongue. I am waiting for you to come to me, to relieve the ache between my thighs.

I hear your feet moving across the concrete floor and then you're so close to me that I can feel your breath across my skin.

'What took you so long?' I ask.

'It'll be worth the wait,' you say.

I feel your hands on my feet. I allow you to lick from heel to arch, over and over again. I feel the wetness of your tongue, the sharpness of your teeth as you bite into my carefully moisturised skin.

A bolt of electricity shoots up my smooth thigh. I inhale deeply as you take each toe into your mouth and suck on it. Then I feel the thick carpet above your sex. I try to take my feet lower but you won't let me. You want to deprive me of sexual pleasure until I'm so hungry that I beg you to take me.

If you could only see the desire in my eyes that I can't allow to reach my lips, for then you would torture me even longer. But I know that in the end I'll get the reward of your cock, your body heavy on top of mine, the taste of you in my mouth and on my skin.

My foot hits the ground with a loud thump. My heartbeat quickens with excited pain. Damn! You are in control and I love it! Okay big daddy, show mama what you got!

Your mouth is on mine, your tongue and teeth pillaging my softness without mercy or restraint. Viciously you take my bottom lip between your teeth and tug. I try to pull away but you grab the sides of my head in your strong hands. Your teeth sink into my top lip. I whimper with pain but between my legs there is nothing but pleasure.

You leave my side for a moment and I'm breathless, wondering what you will do next. Something smooth and soft glides up my thigh. I guess it is a peeled, green banana. In my Caribbean culture green bananas can be turned into delicious dishes but as you dip the tip into my pussy I know that my grandma never had a recipe like this!

The banana circles my large pinkie-sized nipples leaving a wet circle of pussy juice and fruit. Then it's in my mouth and I'm sucking it like it's your dick. I take it deep down my throat. I learned to give head using a green banana. It's still one of my favourite toys. It begins to fall apart under the wetness and passion of my mouth. I sink my teeth into it, swallowing the top half in one smooth gulp. I'd love to devour your cock, to sink my teeth into your military helmet and listen to you scream.

'Please, please eat me!'

Lord, I'm begging already! This darker side of you is making me crazy with desire. Your hands slip between my legs. God you have a big clit, you tell me. It's like a Hershey's kiss.

'But I taste better.'

I hear you smacking your lips. Yes you do, you say. Your hand moves back to my clit.

'Please oh please.'

'Not yet,' you growl and pull your fingers away.

I feel white hot heat next to my face and inhale the aroma of a vanilla scented candle. Now I realize what you are doing. You are planning to fuck me with everything that I've fucked myself with, everything that I've used in place of your hard, jealous cock. I feel my arms drop as you lower my chains and for a moment the sheer relief is almost orgasmic.

Fear sets in as you force me to my knees and push my head down to the ground. Would this new torture be worth the thrill of a slick candle sliding in and out of my pussy? Don't you understand that I need something to fill me when you're not here? Even though my pussy moulds to your dick, it's a naughty, insatiable little slut.

I feel the first drop of hot wax searing my apple shaped ass. I feel it congeal on my skin. Again another drop. This one rolls down my ass cheeks stopping just short of my pussy. Oh, the miserable ecstasy. I want to touch my engorged clit so badly!

'Please, please!'

You pay no attention to the sobbing in my voice. Instead I feel you move away again. Oh God, what will you torture me with next?

I feel warm silicone sliding down my back. I know that you've found my favourite dildo, the one with the added leather straps and buckles. I love to strap it on our bed and ride it hard.

I wait with all holes open and panting, not knowing which one you'll shove my beloved joy into. The snap of the straps across my ass holds more surprise than pain. You've been a bad, bad girl you tell me.

So punish me, punish me until I learn to control myself!

The second swipe is a little harder; the third makes me cry out. I feel my juices flow from my pussy onto the backs of my legs.

'Please let me feel it!'

You place the dildo at the entrance to my pussy. I hold my breath in anticipation. Suddenly the head moves upward and you're forcing it into the tightness of my ass. Holy mother of God! The sweetness of the shaft burrowing deep into my posterior is almost unbearable. You work it inside me, long, deep thrusts that have me scraping my nails on the concrete like a deranged animal.

Desire sweeps through me like wildfire. Brutally you ravage me. I feel your fist on my pussy, kneading me like soft island bread. I grind my hips into your hand.

Without warning the fist and the dildo are gone; I'm left cold, unsatisfied and confused. I call your name softly but you do not answer. Time drags as I wait for your next move.

I hear the drip-drip of our leaky basement tap. Except for that and my heavy breathing there is no sound. Will you leave me here for another few hours? God, I think that I would die from sheer torture and frustration.

And then I feel it. Its rough texture on my ass makes me creamy. I don't need to see it to know that it's beautiful, like hemp, my favourite.

You lift my body until I'm standing up again. Carefully you wind the rope around my chest and stomach in an intricate design that you have perfected over time. I would love to see myself, the pale rope against my dark skin, my big nipples peeking out. The light deprivation is now driving me crazy, but isn't that the point of our little games? You place the rope between my legs, burying it between my pussy lips. It bites into my sensitive clit. The rope travels up between my ass cheeks. It is still sore from the dildo lashing. I love the feel of the rope against my raw flesh. You loop the end of the rope and secure it in a knot.

I adore the feeling of being confined, of being helpless and totally at your mercy. I feel the rope on my nipples. You play with me, teasing me until I can't take it any longer. God, I'm about to come!

Suddenly my blindfold comes off and my face is flooded with light. Even though it is only the softness of candles it is bright after hours of darkness.

I look down and you're on your knees, rubbing the rope against my clit. 'Oh baby, I love the way you love me. Make me come honey, make me scream.' The rope moves faster. 'Oh God, I'm gonna die!'

I bend my knees, opening myself up to you. I can't breathe. I can't think. I can't do anything but feel the texture of the rope and the fire it is causing. At the perfect moment you untie the last knot. I watch in amazement as you scoot under me and open your mouth wide. I'm gushing, my female ejaculation spilling into your open mouth like honey from the rock. I watch you worship at the altar of my cunt.

I am woman, hear me roar as I come.

Oh yes! Yes! Yes!

Just when I think that it's over you run your face up into my pussy. My lips open amazingly releasing even more cream into your hungry mouth, enveloping your nose and mouth in a musky, sticky embrace.

I wish that I could press your head further into my body. I wish that I could grab your cock and shove it into my aching hole. But you know me so well. Sometimes better than I know myself. You stand up and grab my ass cheeks. Then you plunge your stiff, giant cock up into me.

'Who gives you the best fuck?' you ask.

You know that it's you baby, nothing compares to you. Nothing comes close to the feel of your pulsating dick, your warm breath on my skin, the beauty of your contorted face as you come. Oh the taste of your come, nectar from the gods.

Once again you anticipate my needs. You pull out of me and begin rubbing your cock over my rope-clad body. How good that feels.

I drop to my knees and watch you pump your cock above me. I see it coming. Your come erupts like a geyser spewing white liquid gold all over my face. I stick my tongue out and taste the salty tang of your desire.

I love being bad. How about punishing me one more time?

In seconds I'm on my back with my legs spread open with you between them eating my pussy like it's your last supper. God, you're good with that wicked tongue. You eat me, over and over again until I'm reduced to whimpers. Oh yes baby, make me feel like a woman. I love you so much. I need you so much, my sweet baby.

Leg Man
by Landon Dixon

I nodded at the bartender, Matt, and he grinned back at me. Rap music thundered out of the overhanging speakers, shaking the walls of the strip club, egging on a silicon-titted blonde gyrating against the centre stage silver pole. The place was packed for noontime, and the hungry crowd greedily shovelled the three dollar lunch into their faces, as they ogled the balloon-breasted blonde. She held no interest for me, however, not with her chicken legs.

I quickly threaded my way through the cheering and chewing mob, walked down a hall that led to the washrooms, on past the washrooms, and up to a guy leaning against the wall. His thick arms were crossed, and a toothpick balanced precariously between his thick lips. 'Hey, Adam,' I said, my voice breaking.

'Jeff,' the black-clad bouncer responded, eyeing me and smiling. 'Got a new one for you today.'

I rubbed sweaty palms on my pants, sucked cool air into my bursting lungs. 'Y-yeah?'

'Yeah.' He pushed off from the wall, held out his huge right hand, and I promptly crossed his palm with a fifty. He pocketed the cash, then shoved an unmarked door open and stood aside as I walked on through.

It looked like a women's washroom, painted a drab green with white tiling, four cubicles and a couple of sinks lining the far wall. The door whisked shut, and I stood there staring at the first cubicle, my hands trembling, my throat clicking dry when I swallowed. I walked over and pushed the cubicle door open, slipped inside, shot the bolt behind me.

There was no toilet, only a round, padded hole in the wall, waist-level. I fought with my zipper as I gazed at the glory hole, at the yellow shaft of light streaming through from the adjoining room, and then I wrestled my fly down and pulled out my cock. I gripped my rigid dick and moved even closer to the hole, gulped hard and guided my prick through the opening, announcing my presence to whoever was on the other side.

I let go of my rock-hard prong and flattened myself against the wall, sweat prickling my forehead – and nothing happened. The distant thumping of the peeler music sounded from far off, too muted to drown out my ragged breathing. My entire body started shaking, the anticipation and the need growing and growing and growing. And just when I was ready to cry out with angry desire, I heard a slight rustling sound. I braced myself, pressing my lower body hard against the wall and sticking my straining cock out as far as it would go.

I jumped when something brushed against my prick, something soft and smooth and warm – a reply to my greeting. I quickly pulled back, awkwardly got down on my knees, and peered anxiously through the hole at a pair of petite, black-stockinged feet that rested haughtily on the pedestal in the room opposite.

'Yes!' I hissed, licking desert-dry lips, blinking sweat from my eyes, gazing at the most exquisitely-shaped feminine peds I'd ever seen in my life (and I'd seen, and worshipped, plenty of pairs of female feet).

The girl attached to the beautiful feet wriggled her toes at me, and her stockings whispered my name. The delicate, high-arched peds were ivory beneath their sheer, sexy, noir-shaded sheaths, slim and small, perfectly-formed, with slender, succulent toes tipped with medium-long nails painted a shiny crimson. The playful toes waved at me, and my cock grew to epic hardness with the wicked thought of those shapely foot-digits enwrapping and stroking my dick.

I strained to see past the gorgeous pair of feet, to get a glimpse of a luscious leg or two, of the woman beyond, but the well-groomed peds effectively blocked my view, filled my eyes, waved me away; our get-acquainted session was over, it was time to get down to business. I pulled my eyes off those dainty feet and stiffly climbed upright, shoved my painfully-erect cock back through the hole again.

The tender tootsies on the other side of the wall quickly grabbed onto my dick and started brushing up and down the length of it. 'Fuck, yeah!' I groaned into the green paint, revelling in the slick, silky feel of the girl's dextrous feet on my pulsating prong.

I could tell right away that this babe was no amateur, no fumbling footer; her peds weren't thick and clumsy, feet squeezing shaft like they wanted to choke it, toenails scraping sensitive skin, like most girls. No, this lady's feet were soft and gentle, yet firm and controlled. She worked my dick with her feet like she had it in her hands, easily gripping my erection on either side and erotically sliding her silk-clad peds back and forth, giving me the foot-job to end all foot-jobs.

'Yeah,' I murmured, marvelling at the girl's skill. Her talented toes lightly clenched my steely shaft and jacked me repeatedly, the awesome foot friction sending my balls to boil even faster than normal.

There was no holding back this time, no counting to ten or thinking about an ex-mother-in-law – she was that good. I closed my eyes and clawed at the wall and uttered a strangled scream as the wicked pedestrian foot-stroked me to the very precipice of all-out orgasm. Then, right before blast-off, right before white-hot jets of spunk rocket onto the girl's delectable peds, she suddenly pulled her feet away.

'No!' I wailed, pumping my hips and pounding the wall, imploring her not to leave me hanging.

I felt something loop over the base of my raging hard-on, something soft and smooth and warm, like a recently-worn stocking, felt it pulled tight. I opened my eyes – this was something different. Most girls wanted nothing more than to jerk and run, get you to cum and go in a heated rush so they could collect their cash and get back to doing something more respectable, like stripping. But not this lady with the flawless feet; she secured the silken noose around the base of my throbbing rod, cutting off the only escape route for my bubbling semen, then started stroking again, buffing me with her bare feet now, leisurely ped-polishing me without fear of being sprayed with my sticky adulation.

'Fuck almighty!' I yowled, my balls bursting with pressurised jizz, my grossly-engorged dong pulsing with raw, sexual electricity as the barefoot contessa behind the drywall barrier tugged and tugged on my prick.

She swirled her naked feet up and down my cock with more skill than a massage parlour employee with years of hand-job experience, her precious peds stroking my shaft over and over, smooth and sensual and sure-footed, her teasing toes playing all over my prick, grasping my mushroomed hood and squeezing, tickling the super-sensitive spot on the underside of my prong where shaft became head. The silken cock-ring held me in check, prevented me from relieving the thunderous pressure, blowing my load with volcanic intensity. I could only whimper in agony and beg for release, driven to the breaking point and beyond by the girl's delightful, dancing feet.

She thoroughly worked over my angry cock with her fabulous feet, and then – they were gone. 'No, please!' I moaned, an aching, desperate emptiness instantly filling me, my abandoned, stiffened-beyond-stiff cock straining against its silken leash, yearning to be recaptured by the girl's blessed toes.

'Time's up,' someone said.

I glanced at my watch, saw that my time had indeed expired, felt the stocking being untied and pulled from my cock.

'Fuck!' I groaned, ripping my bloated dick out of the hole and wildly fisting it.

But the cum wouldn't come, and when Adam knocked on the cubicle door and said, 'Time's up,' for a second time, I dejectedly tucked my over-stimulated dong back into my pants and exited. If the girl with the gifted, glorious peds was daring me to come back for more, then I was going to meet her dare, because I'd never been so sexually frustrated and exhilarated in all my life.

After feeding him a pair of twenties, Matt-the-day-bartender told me that the new girl with the amazing ped prowess was named Melody, and he agreed to phone me whenever she was on cubicle foot patrol. And that's how it went for a couple of excruciatingly exciting months – Matt would give me a dingle and I'd rush right over, pay my money, and get my granite pole foot-polished by Melody.

She'd toe-stroke me, heel me, put me through the foot-spin, dressed in all manner of ped-apparel: black, red, white, blue, or striped slut-stockings; modest, brown pantyhose; or white, woollen footies with bunny tail balls on the back. Or, best of all, she'd simply jerk me to the jetting point with her bare, brilliant, pedicured feet. I could only stand forward and marvel at her talent, my body shaking uncontrollably, my head spinning, my hands, face, and groin flattened against the sweat-slick wall as she tantalized my numbingly-hard cock with her tender tootsies.

She instinctively knew just when I was about to spill my beans, desecrate her pale, perfect peds with salty, slimy semen, and at that fleeting, failsafe point, she'd instantly bind my dick at its base, corking my eruption, keeping her wondrous feet unblemished, up on the pedestal where they belonged. She'd go on stroking me once the sperm was safely bottled up in my balls, toying with my flaming cock, denying me everything and giving me everything at the same time. And in honour of her grace and beauty and buffing ability, I hadn't cum on my own, or in a woman, since the first day I'd laid dick on Melody's feet.

Eventually, however, I just couldn't take it any more – two months without a jizz-letting, while continually, maddeningly getting ped-dled to the point of sperm-launch, was enough to drive any red-blooded man around the bend and over the edge. So, finally, I asked Matt, verbally and monetarily, if there was any way I could meet face-to-face with the girl with the fantastic feet who was filling my every fantasy. It was against house rules to disclose the identity of the backroom performers to the customers, but Matt bent the rules at the hundred dollar mark.

'See that woman sitting by herself in the balcony?' he said, glancing up, then back down again.

I turned around and quickly spotted the lady in question on the second floor, but the lights were too dim up there for me to get a good look at her. I thanked Matt and walked over to the staircase, took a deep breath, and climbed the stairs.

She was sitting all alone at a table for two, with her back to me, and I stared at her, at her long, black, shimmering hair. Then I rubbed my hands on my pants, briefly touching my rapidly swelling cock for inspiration, and with perspiration prickling my forehead and prick bulging my pants, I quietly came up behind her, reached out a trembling finger, and tapped her on the back.

'H-hi,' I stammered.

She turned to look at me. 'Hi,' she said. Her voice was soft and sweet, her eyes large and violet, her face pretty and pale. A shy smile lifted the corners of her lush, red lips, and she set the drink she'd been holding in her right foot back down on the table.

I gaped at her small, shapely foot, the slender toes that dextrously grasped the highball glass, the medium-long nails flashing a crimson gloss. Then my astonished eyes travelled slowly up from her foot to her shoulders, and I saw that Melody had no arms.

'I was just having a drink,' she said. 'Would you like to join me?' She pushed out a chair with her bare foot.

I snapped back to life. 'Um, I was, uh, wondering if maybe we could go someplace...more private...to talk?'

'You're Jeff, aren't you?' she said, her eyes shining.

'Uh, yeah. How'd you –'

'I recognized your voice.' She looked down at the table. 'I guess I owe you something, don't I, Jeff?'

'Nah,' I scoffed, 'you don't owe me –'

'Yes, I do,' she said firmly.

We both looked at the delicate, ivory foot that gripped the chair, the painted toes playing across the cushion like fingers.

'But I wonder…do you want it now – now that you've seen me?' she asked, shrugging her shoulders.

'I want it anytime you'll give it to me, Melody,' I responded.

She looked up at me and nodded, slipped her foot into a blue slipper that lay on the floor, and stood up and walked past me. I breathed in the warm, intoxicating scent of her perfume, my eyes following the subtle sway of her hips, the sensual swagger of her round butt cheeks in the tight, black skirt she was wearing, the twin flashes of her lithe, white legs. I quickly followed her down the stairs.

'I have a place a couple of blocks from here,' she said when we were outside, standing together on the sun-drenched sidewalk.

I looked down at the tiny girl, studied her pretty face, her petite figure, her smooth, slender legs and slim, shapely ankles, the small slippers that exposed the tops of her delicious feet, and I knew that two blocks were two blocks too far. I was on fire, my cock ready to burst my zipper, my balls boiling with cum. 'I-I can't wait that long,' I mumbled, steering the delicate beauty into an alley that ran between the strip club and the building next door.

She sensed my burning need, as she'd always sensed it in the past, and moaned when I gripped her shoulders and shoved her up against the brick wall, mashed my mouth against hers. We kissed long and hard and hungrily, devouring each other's mouths, before she snaked out her

15

tongue and lashed at my lips. I drove my own tongue into her mouth, and we swirled our slippery, pink stickers together over and over again.

She finally pulled back from my mouth, leaving me gasping, and then broke away and ran down the alley. I cried out for her to stop, frantic that she might be trying to get away from me, deny me my long overdue release yet again – but she wasn't. She jumped up onto a silver garbage can, leaned back against the wall, and kicked off her slippers and cocked a painted toe at me, beckoning at me to join her. I hurried after her, then stood before her and watched in awe as she unhooked my belt and unbuttoned my pants, pulled down my fly and pants with her deft foot-digits.

Then it was her turn to be surprised, as she stared at the twin metal prosthetics that were my legs from the thighs down. 'It's funny, isn't it?' I said, 'a leg man with no legs.'

She looked up into my eyes and smiled. 'I've got all the legs you'll ever need, Jeff.'

She tugged my shorts down, and my swollen dick sprang out into the hot air, twitching with excitement. She quickly grabbed it and started stroking, like she'd stroked me dozens of times before, only this time was really the first time for the both of us.

I closed my eyes and groaned as Melody expertly polished my prick, juggled my balls with one foot while she buffed my dick with the other, completely oblivious to the foot-traffic that passed across the glaring mouth of the alley. She tugged on my jacked-up cock again and again with her nimble, nude feet, and before I could even warn her, the sexual pressure became unbearable, unstoppable, and my balls exploded and I blasted superheated sperm onto her flying feet.

'Yes, Jeff! Coat my feet with your cum!' she yelled, pistoning my spurting cock.

'Fuck almighty!' I bellowed, spraying rope after rope of thick, steaming jizz onto the girl's pumping peds and legs. I came for what seemed like for ever, harder and longer and more voluminously than ever before, my body jerking around like I'd been plugged toe-first into an electrical socket.

And when I was finally, totally spent, Melody took her foot from my wasted dick and brought her peds up to her mouth, tongued my salty, simmering semen off her smeared feet.

'Now it's your turn,' I said, once the footloose girl had licked up and swallowed all of my goo.

She smacked her glazed lips and grinned at me, then unfastened her skirt and pulled it open, arched her back and flung it aside. She spread her supple legs, exposing her glistening pussy. 'This what you're looking for?' she asked.

'Exactly,' I replied, grabbing her lean, lightly-muscled legs around the ankles and kissing and licking and biting her fleshy calves, her well-turned ankles, her magnificent feet. Then I shouldered her dancer's legs and jammed two of my fingers into her sopping wet twat, started sliding them rapidly back and forth.

'Yes, Jeff! Yes!' she shrieked, wrapping her feet around my neck, jamming her drenched pussy into my pumping digits.

I added another finger to the first two and relentlessly pounded her poon, finger-fucked her into oblivion, the leggy foot fatale closing her eyes and arching her body and screaming as she came in a heated gush.

'We were meant for each other,' I gasped, once Melody's wild cries of ecstasy had stopped ricocheting off the walls of the alley, as we both tongued her tangy cum off my fingers. 'We fit together perfectly.'

Watching
by Oya

Frank watched her from his window every day. Her apartment was a floor above and across the alleyway, so he was looking up at her when she worked in her kitchen.

She often had on shorts or a little skirt and sometimes just panties. He dreamed of tying her up with rope. She would be so helpless and vulnerable and beautiful. He could do whatever he wanted to her.

One night he looked up and she was getting spanked right there in her kitchen as she washed dishes. A large man yanked her light pink panties up the crack of her ass and spanked her round beautiful tan cheeks.

Frank stayed in the dark so they wouldn't notice him watching. It seemed like the man was yelling at her as he slapped her ass. Then he pulled off her panties, got on his knees and buried his face between her ass cheeks.

It blew Frank's mind. He felt his cock aching and just had to unzip his pants and take his throbbing cock into his hand.

The man stood up; his finger disappeared into her ass. She squirmed and he grabbed her long black hair, bending her head back and licking her neck.

Again and again he rammed his finger in and out of her. Then he pushed her over the sink, took his cock and pushed it into her ass.

Even at this distance, he heard her squeal and saw her jerk. The man showed no mercy, fucking her in the ass until she fucked him back.

Frank loved the transformation – seeing her resist at first and then pushing her ass to meet the man's cock. He could hear the man calling her a whore and a slut and telling her to take it up the ass like she needed it.

It was just too much! Frank came before either of the two in the window did.

He liked watching her. Another night when he got in late, he went to his kitchen to get a drink of water and didn't turn on the light. Glancing up he saw his hot neighbour getting felt up by a much older man. The man was wearing a suit; she was dressed in a skirt and blouse.

He was shorter than her, his head barely reaching her chin. He had her up against the fridge. He was opening her blouse and she was pushing him away, but not too vigorously. She seemed to let him overpower her until her black bra was exposed.

Once he had her tits exposed he sucked on one and fondled the other.

All the fight had gone out of her; she was leaning back against the fridge, her eyes closed and her mouth open.

The older man sucked each tit in turn, then removed his belt and lightly tapped each nipple.

Flinging the belt aside, he put one hand over her mouth and his other hand between her legs under her skirt.

He must have known what he was doing under there because she put her arms around him and rubbed her tits in his face.

She lay back on the table and he pushed up her skirt, leaned between her legs and licked her pussy.

Frank gasped. He could see her dark bush, and at the same time the look of ecstasy on her face.

He thought about his naughty neighbour a lot and kept watching. He badly wanted to tie her up and spank her. She definitely deserved it – and she liked it. He wanted to belt her and show her to other horny men. He wanted to fuck her face with his hard cock while she was helpless and bound. He wanted to taste her and fuck her pussy. But Frank was a gentleman. He wouldn't do any of those things to a woman unless she gave him a sign indicating she wanted it too.

He thought about approachable women. Carmen at his job seemed to be flirting with him lately, but he took the view that it was crazy to start anything with someone you worked with.

But the right woman had to be out there.

With high hopes he went for a drive and stopped for a few beers at a bar downtown. For a weeknight, it was pretty full and friendly, so he decided to play some pool.

He won the game against some guy, couldn't stop thinking about his neighbour. That was when he saw her. She was standing there waiting to play the next game with him.

His eyes stood out on stalks at a very hot-looking woman in a red blouse, her nipples brash and brazen through the cloth.

She wore tight black jeans and high-heeled shoes. Her long blonde hair was in a braid and her eyes were as big as Bambi.

Her heat was enough to burn a guy. Frank let her break, his heat rising as she bent over the table.

'Loser gets spanked or gets a drink,' he said, his gaze fixed on her ass.

He almost blew a fuse when she smiled at him over her shoulder. 'We'll see which seems better at the time,' she said, wiggling her ass suggestively.

With the stakes that high, Frank played his ass off. He made damned sure she never got to shoot again.

'What are ya drinking?' he asked, not daring to push his luck and go straight for the spanking.

She was sipping her drink when the subject came back up.

'Consolation prize?' she said, raising her glass. 'So! When do I get the spanking?'

'Do you mean that?'

'I am asking.'

Blood racing, he asked her if she'd ever gotten a good spanking by a man.

'What do you think?' she asked playfully. 'Come on. Do I look the shy, retiring type?'

This was too good to be true. 'I think you need one.'

He put his arm around her waist. 'Nice body.'

In response, she wriggled and complained of feeling hot.

With trembling fingers, he undid two of her blouse buttons and blew on her cleavage.

'That cooler?'

She let her head fall back, sighed and smiled.

'It helps. But hell, I'm naturally hot. Hot as hell.'

Frank touched her tits through her blouse. She smiled encouragingly even though she was as aware as he was that they were being watched.

The bartender came over and suggested they might prefer more privacy in the back.

Frank thanked him, and throwing a smile at those showing an interest, he escorted his sexy lady into a room set aside from the bar and furnished with a big, green sofa.

He kissed her and unbuttoned all her blouse buttons, baring her bra-less tits with their big nipples and creamy complexion.

He told her how great they were then lowered his head, sucking on them one at a time.

She moaned, enveloped his face with her tits to the point that he had to come up for air, and stroked his head.

'This is all very well,' she said in a husky voice, 'but what about my spanking. I lost the game, remember?'

It was difficult to pull his head away from her tits, but he forced himself.

'You are a hot horny little slut aren't you?' he gasped.

She let him lay her across his lap face down and wriggled seductively when he spanked her real hard.

Her squirming and squealing attracted the attention of several men from the bar. They appeared in the doorway just as Frank stood her up and undid her jeans, pulling them down to expose her lovely ass.

Resisting her beautiful bush, he pulled her back down across his lap and spanked her bare ass in front of the other men. She pretended she didn't know they were being watched, but he knew she did, knew she was enjoying it.

After a firm spanking he stood her up and gave her a nice licking while he remained seated, his hands gripping her ass so he could more easily pull her toward his face.

As he licked her clit, she moved her pussy to his tongue eagerly.

The men who were watching could no longer remain quiet. 'She likes what you're giving her.'

They whistled and egged him on.

He made her get down on the floor on all fours with her blouse open and her jeans down at her thighs. Her white ass in the dim room was a fantastic sight. Frank took off his belt and used it on the hot woman's round behind in front of the small audience they had. He landed his black leather belt across her ass until she tried to crawl away from him. Grabbing her by her braid, he made her suck his cock. While he sat on the sofa, she remained on her knees between his legs, his hands using her braid like a pulley to push and pull at her head.

Wanting to delay his climax, Frank put her back across his lap and penetrated her ass hole with his finger. She whimpered. He fingered her ass and told her he wanted to take her home and tie her up and then fuck her everywhere – in her mouth, her cunt, her big fine ass. He told her he might decide to keep her tied up in his house for days as his slave. He rammed her ass as he said that and she lifted it to meet his finger.

Their audience began to ask to join in. That was something he could well do without.

'Come on. Let's get out of here.'

She went willingly; hot to have more of him and lingering on the brink of climax.

In his apartment, he made her strip and he tied her up, just as he'd watched his neighbour doing.

He pulled the rope tightly around her tits and thighs so that she couldn't move her hands. Her thighs were apart and her tits restricted by the time he was done.

He asked her if she minded being photographed. She told him to get on with it.

He photographed her on the bed like that, and then licked her clit until she came on his tongue.

His game wasn't ended. Not yet.

Her eyes widened when he scolded her. 'You got naked for a strange man. You are a horny little bitch. You made the men in the bar crazy. I could have let them loose on you. But I decided to punish you myself. You will be my slave tonight. You will call me Master. If you feel pain, you deserve it. You will obey me and try your utmost to please me, whatever that entails. You are my slut, and I like you bound and helpless. You need to learn a lesson about torturing men.'

He sat on a chair and stared at his hostage. She was quite a sight and he couldn't possibly leave her unmolested, not with his dick still stiff in his pants.

He got up and went to her, nibbling on her tits until her nipples were very hard. While she remained bound in his rope and on his bed, he climbed on her and fucked her cunt from behind, yanked her by her hair and called her a whore, a hot slut, a horny bitch, a brazen hussy.

He told her she was his bitch and she was going to like being his bitch. He told her she was going to be naked for days and at his service. He fucked her hard and told her that her pussy was delicious and hot and juicy. He told her she liked getting fucked because she was a whore.

She answered him, telling him to give her more, not to stop.

'I love being so overpowered. It's so hot.'

'Had it done before?'

He gasped as he said it, fucking her for all he was worth.

She told him of her summers with her Uncle Lou and how he'd sneak into the bathroom when she showered and try to do things. She had acted like she didn't want it, but she'd left the latch off purposely.

At night he sometimes climbed into bed with her. She was only 17, and he would pull down her baby doll panties under the covers and turn her over onto her stomach. He would play with her ass and push his finger into her tight ass hole. She would gasp and act like she was going to cry and Uncle Lou would cover her mouth and tell her she needed something. He told her she was walking around in skimpy clothes all day asking for it. He told her he wouldn't get her in trouble if she accepted her discipline from him. One night 'discipline' meant she had to show her pussy to his friend. She had to act like it was accidental, but she had to be sure his friend saw her naked between her legs. Uncle Lou threatened her with a much worse punishment if she didn't do as she was told. And he reminded her it was her own fault for being such a bad girl. She'd never disclosed that she'd liked what she was doing, that although he thought she was in his power, showing her naked pussy to appreciative older men, he was really in hers. She liked what she was doing.

Frank pulled out of her cunt and came on her ass, the come dribbling down between her full cheeks.

Once he was sated, he untied her and directed her to shower. They ate, they drank, and later he tied her up again. It was different this time although still intricate. This time he tied one of her legs to the leg of his kitchen table. He also tied her hands together in front of her and made her stay bent over the kitchen table for a while.

'I want everyone to see you.'

He put his kitchen light on, stood behind her and stared at her ass; drank another beer; lit a joint and held it for her when it was her turn to inhale.

'Slut?'

'Yes, Master?'

She shivered with apprehension when she said it.

'I'm going to fuck you up the ass.'

His cock was hard again just from looking at her.

The kitchen light glared, so he turned it off and lit candles so anyone outside could see her getting fucked up the ass.

'A little punishment, just to remind you of your place in this.'

He took his belt and whipped her ass a few times until she yelled.

'Now you are goin' to get it, bitch.'

Separating her cheeks, he guided his cock until he was easing himself inside her tight hot ass hole. The feeling was electric. His cock was being squeezed and at the same time sucked into her ass.

Her ass cheeks shook some when he rammed inside her. 'You like it, bitch? Huh? You like getting my cock up your ass, bitch!?'

'Ow, it hurts,' she whined.

It was a put-on. He could tell that by the way her ass was wriggling, pushing back against him.

But he knew what she wanted. He responded with a whack of the belt. 'How's that? Does that hurt?'

Tied down and taken, she pushed her ass up to meet his cock. He sensed she knew it would inspire more beating.

He grunted and belted her as he came in her tight hot ass, until eventually he had no more to give and the woman herself collapsed, exhausted, beneath him.

Frank remained slumped over her body for a few minutes, but as he began to disengage himself, he happened to look upwards. His neighbour was at the window touching herself as she watched him, just as he'd used to do.

Andrea And Monique
by N. Vasco

'Rene and I broke up' Monique told me as she stirred her coffee. I was checking my make-up and nearly smeared the lipstick all over my face when she said this.

I never did like Rene for her: Beautiful and handsome yes, but too involved with his own good looks. I can't bear that type but, then again, Monique and I are different in so many ways. She rarely wears make-up while I prefer a bolder look. Her high cheekbones, lovely slanted eyes, whiskey lips and sandy hair come from a Chinese mother and Dutch father. I got my black hair and alabaster complexion from a Latin and Greek background. Her slender figure is the result of a successful dance career. My body is more hourglass, the type people call voluptuous. She maintains a year-round tan, wears loose dresses without a slip and enough jewellery for a gypsy. My office job calls for skirts and high heels.

I tend to keep to myself while Monique expresses every idea that comes into her mind. One afternoon we visited an antiquities museum that featured statues from ancient Mycenae. Women back then wore dresses that displayed their ample breasts and adorned their faces with very provocative make-up.

'That's you!' Monique exclaimed, drawing looks from the other patrons as she pointed to a statue of a voluptuous, bare-breasted priestess wearing lots of make-up. Even her nipples were painted a lovely shade of carmine that contrasted nicely with her alabaster skin.

'Why!' Monique said. 'Your breasts are bigger than hers!'

I wanted to hush her but after one of the stuffy old matrons who volunteered in the museum give us a dirty look, we broke out in giggles and quickly stepped into another room filled with statues from India. We were alone in that room, the only sound the taps of my high heels and Monique's sandals echoing off the walls.

'Oh, look,' Monique said as she admired a statue of a Hindu dancer, the curves of her generous hips and rounded breasts exaggerated by her provocative, dancer's pose.

'There you are again.' Monique cooed as her eyes ran over every detail of the statue until she was looking at the rather large nipples that sat on top of each breast. Then, she looked at me before grabbing my hand, standing me next to the statue and saying; 'Do the same pose, please, just for me!' while taking out her camera.

I could never say no to Monique. I guess by now you must realize I was always very attracted to her, even back in the days when we met at the University of Paris. So, I looked at the statue for a minute, kicked off my shoes and struck the same pose.

'Now take off your top!'

I responded with a loud 'No!' followed by more loud giggles, drawing the attention of the dour-faced matron who entered the room and told us to leave.

'Maybe you should try to get laid once in a while. Then you wouldn't be so uptight,' Monique said as I pulled my shoes back on. I could see the matron's face turn a beetroot red as the words sputtered in her mouth; before she could say another word I took Monique's hand and got out of the museum as fast as possible.

That's my lovely Monique, always making heads turn wherever she goes; and today was no exception.

We always meet in the same café for lunch and when I looked up to watch her enter I was treated to wonderfully teasing glimpses of her provocative figure through the light cotton dress she wore, as she passed the window. We had always exchanged light, friendly kisses but this time she paused, stroked my arm and complimented me on my outfit.

'You always look so professional, yet so sexy,' she said, gazing at me. 'That skirt really shows off your figure.' I didn't know what to say. Like I said, I had always harboured feelings for Monique, sometimes masturbating long into the night and fantasizing about kissing her lovely, heart-shaped lips. But I valued our friendship even more and kept them a secret, even forcing a casual attitude when I heard about the break-up.

I took a deep breath and asked 'Weren't you two planning on getting married?'

'I had suggested it once,' she responded, buttering a croissant. 'But, really, could you see that happening? Remember last summer?'

I nodded. I was dating one of my co-workers back then, a handsome American named Bob. The four of us made plans to spend a weekend at a seaside cottage. At the last moment Bob was called back to America and I wound up by myself at the train depot. Monique consoled me by offering to go shopping for a swimsuit. The thought of seeing her lovely figure in a skimpy bikini made me feel a little better.

The sales girl at the shop was a lovely Polynesian girl called Claire who wore an alluring one-piece that barely hid her round breasts and firm buttocks. She selected a yellow thong bikini that showed off Monique's wonderful tan.

Both of them convinced me to try on the same style, but in black. 'It'll look wonderful against your skin,' Monique said as I changed in the fitting room.

I stepped out to their approving comments, and couldn't help the rush of excitement coursing through my body. The mirror next to the dressing room reflected my almost naked body, standing close to those two beautiful women in skimpy bikinis.

The admiring looks Claire gave me, and Monique's playful slapping of my exposed buttocks almost sent me into an orgasm. I wanted to run my mouth all over their luscious bodies, kiss their lips and taste their juices.

Thinking back, I believe Monique could sense my arousal. She kept on stroking my hair while Claire rang up our purchases at the counter.

'Well, well,' was Rene's comment when I stepped onto the deck with Monique, both of us all but naked in our tiny swimsuits. The three of us were on a yacht lent by one of his wealthy clients. He looked so handsome at the wheel with his tanned sculpted chest. I guess he was unused to seeing me so exposed and kept eyeing me as he steered the boat. Monique had to constantly warn him to watch out for the nearby jetties, all the while enduring his almost ridiculous attention to my body.

This lasted for only a few minutes. We passed by a jetty where two blonde, English girls were sunning themselves. Rene slowed the boat down when he saw they were topless and began chatting with them in a very flirtatious manner. The sight of their nubile bodies glistening with suntan oil made my gaze linger for a while until I noticed the hurt expression on Monique's face. I knew she tolerated Rene's attitude, but this was too much.

After a while he got discouraged and set off, not even wondering why Monique was so quiet. We turned down his invitation to go snorkelling, opting to sunbathe instead.

After he left Monique asked me to put lotion on her. I rubbed her lithe, hard body for while, my hands massaging her firm shoulders, taut back and tiny waist until I heard her murmur 'Please do my buttocks.'

Those words made my pulse surge in my ears. I paused for a moment, forgetting the hot afternoon sun on my back, the sound of the waves against the hull and the smell of the ocean in my nostrils. Monique shifted a little, causing the delicious swell of her buttocks to arch up ever so invitingly. I tipped the bottle of lotion over the twin hills of her backside and let the oil slowly pour over her naked skin, even allowing some of it to seep into the cleft where her thong disappeared.

I heard Monique murmur and coo and, when I began to rub and kneed the firm, hard muscles of her glorious buttocks, she began to moan between short gasps. I was in my glory, my hands drinking in her buttocks, thighs and hips until she suddenly turned around and asked me to do her front.

It was wonderful rubbing her backside but the sight of her upright breasts, defined stomach and naked hips sent my heart racing again. I wanted to take my top off and let my generous bosoms ooze all over her taut breasts and hard nipples. To part her thighs, bury my face in her pussy and drink the juices of her body.

Just then, she looked at me. I could see the hurt in her eyes and knew it was caused by Rene's boorish attitude. I wanted to hold her, to kiss those lovely lips and make her feel totally appreciated.

Suddenly, we heard Rene clamber back on board. Monique quickly sat up, a confused look on her face. I was afraid she didn't know how to deal with my attention. Rene was oblivious to everything. The sight of his gymnast physique glistening in the bright sunshine made him look like a Greek god. He gave us each a big smile before reaching into a pocket and showing Monique a gold, heart-shaped charm on a chain.

'I wanted to give you this later but decided maybe now would be a good time' he said, putting the chain around her neck. Monique responded with a slight smile. 'I'm sorry for my behaviour back there.' She even gave him a brief hug and endured a friendly pat on her lovely, bare behind. It was a scene played out over and over again. I know she even sensed his eyes travelling all over my body as he held her.

We had a light, quiet dinner at the cottage. Rene was still talking about his underwater adventure as he openly fondled and caressed Monique's body. She seemed in a better mood. I decided to give them some time alone and went to my room.

I looked at my reflection in my mirror and liked what I saw. The tiny white lines on my hips and the contrast between my dark breasts and the pale triangles that surrounded my nipples made a wonderfully sexy look. I held my breasts and licked my nipples. Bob had introduced me to this technique but all I could think of was Monique's delicate tongue stimulating my breasts.

Just to be daring, I tried on one of the wispy cotton dresses she had in the closet. The white, almost see-through material contrasted nicely with my cinnamon dark skin, giving a provocative view of the white thong I wore

33

underneath. I looked out the window, saw it was a beautiful, moonlit night. I knew I would probably spend a good part of the night masturbating but decided I needed a walk first. Maybe it would cool me down.

I went downstairs and sure enough, Monique and Rene were kissing on the living room couch, the fireplace casting a sensual glow on the entire room. Rene for once was the gentleman but Monique whistled and teased me as I went to the door. I blew them each a kiss, put on my sandals and stepped out.

It was pleasant walking along the water's edge. I tried to distract myself from the day's disturbing events by staring out at the dark ocean, illuminated by early moonlight. It was no use. Remembering how beautiful Monique's dainty feet looked in her sandals, the kind Hindu women wear, open-toed, with a slight heel, or her almost naked body glistening with suntan lotion made my heart race. I never noticed until that day but Rene had such handsome thighs. Thinking of his strong buttocks and manly calves brought a moist sensation between my legs. I passed by a series of dunes and remembered Claire's lovely cinnamon skin and her upright breasts. Polynesian women have such lovely figures. And then there were those two English girls, sunning their young, pale bodies on the jetties.

Suddenly, I heard a light, feminine giggle from behind one of the dunes. I walked as quietly as possible until I saw two figures wrapped in a blanket sitting in front of a small fire. They were close enough to be kissing. A sigh followed by a brief yet pleasant moan followed.

My curiosity got the better of me and before I knew it I was close enough for my eyes to adjust the dim glow. When they parted I saw to my pleasant surprise that it was the two young English girls we had seen earlier. Suddenly, the blanket fell to the sand, revealing their newly tanned skin, contrasting with the white, threadbare bikinis on their nubile bodies. They sat there for a while, looking into each other's eyes as they stroked and caressed each other's arms, pert breasts and trim, youthful stomachs. I could hear their conversation.

'I never kissed a girl before. I liked it' one said while running her hands through the other's long blonde hair.

'I think you'll like this better?' the other girl said as she kneeled, parted her lover's thighs and buried her face in her crotch. I imagined what it would be like, my mouth travelling over the slight fabric of her tiny briefs, my tongue pushing the material aside before tasting the juices of her loins, mixed with the flavour of the ocean still on her body.

I realized my hands had wandered underneath my dress and were stroking my nipples as I saw the girl who was enjoying her lover's oral attention reach up to undo her top. I ached to see her tight breasts and pert nipples but, just then, a loud voice called from nearby.

'Phoebe! Nicole! We're leaving now.'

The girls parted quickly. They gathered their blanket and put out the fire. I heard them exchange a few words as they walked away.

'They're going out to dinner. Do you want to go with them or stay in the cottage?'

'What do you think?'

I heard them giggle and saw their departing silhouettes embrace tenderly.

Disappointed, I went back to the cottage. The walk did nothing to calm me down.

When I reached the cottage I heard a moan through one of the open windows. It was torture but I decided to look anyway.

35

I nearly moaned out loud myself when I peered through the open blinds and saw Monique, her tanned body glowing in the firelight, on her knees taking Rene's handsome cock between her beautiful lips. Both were naked, their perfect bodies glowing in the firelight. I could even hear Rene gasp as Monique ran her tongue all over his shaft, nibble his glans and suck greedily at his balls. I closed my eyes as my hands went at it again, travelling all over my body, probing my wet, aching pussy, rubbing my breasts and nipples.

I opened my eyes in time to see them change positions. By now, Monique was crouched on all fours, showing the inviting curve of her buttocks to Rene as he knelt and whispered something in her ear. She smiled and nodded. I wondered what they said but was overtaken by the expression on Monique's face. A craving, almost hungry, expression as Rene entered her from behind and began thrusting. She shut her eyes and opened her mouth wide. Her expression was one of total desire and satisfaction. Of sheer abandonment and total ecstasy. Of…

'Andrea, are you listening to me?'

Monique's voice brought me back to the cafe. My panties were moist. I had to wipe off a bead of perspiration from my forehead. She held my hand. The touch of her delicate, jewelled fingers did nothing to stop my heart from racing.

'Tell me' I said, trying to look casual 'Did you and Rene ever have anal sex?'

A coy, demure look crossed her face. My mind went back to the cottage. Rene entering her from behind while she gasped and smiled with a deep, hungry look.

'Yes,' she replied 'Many times. It's such a wonderful feeling. A delicious balance between pain and pleasure. And the orgasm that comes from it is so…unique.'

She sat back and toyed with one of her necklaces. I noticed the charm was missing.

'Did you get rid of that charm?' I asked, my hands trembling as I stirred my coffee.

She smiled and said 'Do you remember my aunt Mathilde?'

'The one who passed away last year? We went to the funeral,' I responded. Monique's family had a rather low opinion of Mathilde. A burlesque dancer who married a rich man and became a jet-setting libertine.

'The inheritance finally came through,' she said while buttering another croissant.

'You got the country house?' I asked. But what this did have to do with the charm?

'I went there this weekend. To clear my mind,' she said, a look of satisfaction on her face that didn't come from the croissant. She ran her lovely fingers over those beautiful lips. My heart raced. I knew this story was going to be…unique.

'I got the deeds and two keys from her solicitor.' Monique began. 'It was a long drive to the house. She lived as a recluse in her latter years. Her only company was a lovely Vietnamese maid who had been with her since her days in burlesque. Her name was Mai. I heard she passed away a few months after Mathilde.'

'The first key allowed me into her house. There was such a lush cosiness to the entire place. Opulent Persian rugs and antique furniture. I had meant to leave before dark but after seeing her boudoir I changed my mind.'

'What was so special about it?'

She gave me a wicked smile and said 'You should see it. All lace and ruffles, a lace canopy over the bed, nude statuettes of men and women everywhere...and her pictures.'

'Pictures?'

'She was beautiful!' Monique almost shouted. 'Wonderful black and whites of her in see-through lace, feather boas, exotic costumes. Some were of her totally nude. What a body! Her breasts were as nice as yours.'

She was eyeing my chest by then. I wanted to rip my blouse off and feel those lips on my nipples. I controlled myself, gave her a light pat on the hand and said; 'Go on.'

'She had lots of costumes in the house. Trunks and closets with all kinds of things. But I was curious. The first key opened the gate and all the locks in the house. I searched the big closet in her bedroom and found a steamer trunk. The second key fit perfectly in it. Inside was one set of black silk stockings and five big photo albums. There were more sexy pictures of Mathilde except she wasn't alone in any of them.'

'You mean?' I whispered, my throat was dry by then. I wanted to hear more.

'I saw her with one, two, sometimes three men at once. All making love to each mouth of her body. Her expressions ranged from playful to completely orgasmic. There were even pictures of her and Mai. A petite, curvy, high-breasted beauty with full, sensuous lips. They made love in many ways. Sometimes with their mouths, other times with these ivory phalluses...'

We giggled at this. I loosened the top button of my blouse. This resulted in a sexy expression on her face. I wondered. What was she thinking of? I decided to play for time and asked 'Who took the pictures?'

'Oh,' Monique replied, 'Mai's lover, I guess. One picture showed Mathilde behind a camera wearing only those black stockings while Mai and a handsome Latin man were on a bed having anal sex.'

'How did you know it was him?' I asked.

'There's a picture of him bare-chested and standing next to a camera in Mai's room. He had broad shoulders and deep, mysterious eyes. Suddenly, I had the urge to take off my clothes and wear her stockings. I wanted to lie in her bed and masturbate with those pictures all around me. I must've had ten orgasms before going to sleep. But that wasn't the end of it.

'You see, I had this wonderful dream. I was in her room, still wearing only the stockings. Lit candles everywhere. There was a perfumed scent in the room, like jasmine. A door opened. Mai entered wearing a long, black dress with waist-high slits that exposed her shapely thighs. She sat on the bed, poured oil in her hands and rubbed my feet. I felt completely at ease and closed my eyes as her expert hands gently but firmly worked up my ankles, calves and thighs. She rubbed my hips and stomach and then stopped. I opened my eyes and saw her undo that beautiful dress. She straddled my body, poured oil on her breasts and ran those sexy, hard nipples all over me. Every inch of my skin tingled with electricity.

'After a while she got up, turned me over and rubbed more oil on her body. I lay on my stomach as she ran her nipples all over my back and began licking the cleft of my buttocks, all the way down to my anus. The feeling of that tongue reaming my back door! It's so nice to feel a penis in there but the sensation of that lovely mouth! She poured more oil over my back. It flowed down my cleft while her fingers entered my anus and pussy. I came right away, my entire body flowed with orgasm after orgasm.

'Then she gave me a light kiss and led me to another room. Her lover was there, shirtless and loading film into a big, old-fashioned camera pointing to a low bed.

'I sat down as she adjusted my make-up and brushed my hair. She went back to her lover who started taking pictures of me. Then I heard another door open. To my pleasant surprise I saw three handsome, naked men enter the room. Their bodies were trim and athletic. They surrounded me on the bed, their stiff members brushing against my body. I decided right then to give the best performance anyone had ever seen. I leaned down and opened my mouth wide, taking each throbbing cock in my mouth. I never made love to more than one man at a time but I wanted all of them at once.

'I realized right then I was the one in control. They were there to please me. I pushed one man down to my crotch and enjoyed his oral attention. His tongue licked my wet, flowing pussy. The other two soon followed, licking my anus and nipples. Their mouths brought on yet another orgasm that shook my body with pleasure.

'I wanted to return the favour. I told one to lie down, straddled him and slid his wonderful cock into my wet pussy. It felt so good, his thick meat sliding inside my body. I turned my head, took the nearest penis in my mouth and sucked and licked away. I still wanted more. I gestured to the last man and raised my buttocks slightly. He understood, knelt behind me and slid his cock into my anus which Mai had so thoughtfully lubricated.

'Oh, to make love to these three beautiful men at once. To feel every orifice of my body filled with hard, veined manhood. It was so…wonderful. They began to moan in unison. I sucked even harder as my hips and buttocks moved back and forth. I wanted them to come right away.

Suddenly, I felt their bodies tense as they emitted one final, masculine shout and came inside me.

'Suddenly, juicy, glorious cum bathed my pussy, came down my throat and filled my anus. I felt every inch of my being filled to the rim with hot, creamy, liquid manhood. It was wonderful.

'Suddenly, I woke up alone in the bed but I could still feel the sensation of having a cock in each of my three mouths. I sat up. My hand travelled over my neck and I felt Rene's locket. I looked at it for a second, tore it off and flung it through an open window.'

We sat in silence for a while. Monique's dream flowed through my mind like a river. This was it. I had to ask her.

'Monique, I…don't know how to say this but…' I stammered. She held my hand. It was now or never. 'Would you like to make love to me?' that was it. I didn't know what to expect.

She leaned close and whispered in my ear 'I've wanted to make love to you since that afternoon on the boat. Do you remember?'

I nodded, happy and excited at the turn our relationship was about to take.

'Let's go to the house,' she said; 'I'd like to show you the pictures.'

That evening we lay naked on her aunt's bed, our arms and legs wrapped around each other after the most intense love-making I had ever enjoyed. In a moment of sheer abandonment we had even licked and fingered each other's back doors. I could still feel her delicate fingers inside my anus while her other fingers probed and stroked my pussy. It was so new to me.

'That was wonderful.' She said, cupping my breast. She had fondled them all day.

'Yes, it was,' I responded while her palms rubbed my nipples.

'I still like being with a man, though,' she said. 'I mean, the right kind of man.'

I smiled at her caution. 'Me too. I guess I could never be exclusive.'

I mused at the thought. To lie between Monique and another handsome man, to feel her mouth on my loins as I enjoyed a hard, veined penis in my mouth.

'But what if we each find the right man?' I said, enjoying her fingers on my nipples.

Her delicate face seemed aroused by the thought. She gave me a sly smile and said 'Foursome.'

I held her close.

'But tell me, are you in any hurry?'

She gave me a sly smile and said 'Not really'.

We laughed and made love until we both fell asleep.

The Big Bang
by Lynn Lake

When Joe Coup saw the bright lights on the dark, lonely logging road up ahead, he stomped the brakes and banged the steering wheel.

'Hell's bells!' he growled.

The brilliant, vertical beam of pure, white light swept up the dirt road towards his battered pick-up truck. He slammed into reverse, stomped the accelerator. The vehicle shot backwards, jouncing crazily over water-filled potholes, Joe's head ricocheting off the bare metal roof, clamping his hardhat down like a bottle cap.

The speedometer needle quivered up to fifty then fell like a tree. The beam of light had suffused the truck, capturing it and the cursing lumberjack, stopping the both of them dead. The roof peeled back like the lid on a sardine can, and Joe was airborne. His indignant profanity filled the pine-scented night air, startling wolves and shocking chipmunks.

'What'd you want this time?' Joe groused, cantilevering his fingers under his hardhat and popping it off, freeing up his brains.

He was standing in a spaceship miles above the Earth's surface, glaring at a glowing orange sphere hovering eye-level in front of him. An alien life form of pure energy, he grudgingly assumed.

'I'm over here,' came the reply, in perfect, if squeaky, English.

Joe looked down, way down, at a green, two-inch long centipede-like creature on the metallic floor of the spacecraft.

The creature arched its head, waved ten or twelve arms or legs in universal greeting. 'That's our light and heating unit,' it explained, pointing still more appendages at the orange sphere. 'My name's Kazar.'

Joe looked back up at the glowing ball, like he preferred it. 'This is the sixth time I've been abducted,' he complained, 'and I'm starting to get pissed off.'

The first three times had been interesting, fun even, the cold probing offset by the warm and fuzzy half-hour of fame: guest appearances on the television shows Unexplained Unknowns and PSI: Oregon, guest-of-honour spots at science fiction conventions and NASA fundraisers, a ghost-written bestseller-in-the-Nevada-Area 51 entitled ET Loves Me.

But the celebrity had faded like the prospects of an ALF reunion movie anytime soon, after the fourth abduction. And by the fifth, the 'kook' label had been firmly affixed. He lost his long-suffering girlfriend and his plum job at her father's sawmill, moved into an abandoned Airstream trailer on the edge of an acid lake in the middle of a clear-cut nowhere, only his hand and a satellite dish to keep him company, chainsawing and trimming and hauling logs, freelance, for a living.

He was the guy who cried 'Watch the skies!' once too often, Chicken Little in a spacesuit, and now no one was listening – except the tiny green centipede with the Mickey Mouse voice.

'This will be the final time,' Kazar assured him. 'For this,' it gestured expansively with almost all its limbs, 'is the mother ship.'

'And what were all the other spaceships – kiddie cars?' Joe grumbled.

Kazar grinned, then scuttled over to an inch-high instrument panel and peered out of a BB-sized porthole, pressing a button to correct the trajectory of the flying saucer. One of its limbs inadvertently triggered the hyper-light drive which sent it splatted against the porthole. The sudden speed sent Joe flying.

Kazar shut down the drive and apologized, as Joe climbed angrily to his feet. 'The others were merely…exploratory vessels,' it said, continuing their discussion. 'Equipped to search for the man who will serve our peoples' purposes – serve the place purposes of peoples in all…uh, serve the purposes of all places and…'

Joe snorted, ran a rugged hand through his shaggy, blonde hair.

'And you are that man, Joe,' Kazar said, 'and this ship contains the most precious of all cargoes.'

Joe defiantly spat a line of black tobacco at the floor, splashing little Kazar in the wash. 'I'm not doin' nuthin' for you guys! I've had it! I'm all sampled and studied…out! You guys can go crawl back into your black hole and pull it in after…'

He stopped his tirade when Kazar snapped its limbs and a being as beautiful as a billion sunsets suddenly appeared, naked as the break of day. 'Mother!' Kazar squeaked triumphantly.

Joe's fists unfurled and he gulped his chaw, ogled the woman with the stars in her eyes.

'She's everything you've ever dreamed of, Joe,' Kazar piped, standing up on its hind limbs and gesturing at the heavenly creature. 'A composite of your ideal woman come to life, assembled from mind probes of your once-every-ten-seconds sexual fantasies.'

Joe had to admit she was built, alright. He brushed splinters off his dirty Hard-On Wood Products t-shirt and finger-combed his scruffy beard.

Kazar glanced at a data screen the size of a pinkie toenail. 'She has, uh, Diane Lane's feet and legs, Jenny Lopez's rear end, Pamela Lee Anderson's...uh, Pamela Anderson Lee's...'

'Pamela Anderson,' Joe breathed.

'Right, yes. Pamela Anderson's chest. Jenny Connelly's face and Jenny Aniston's hair. And, uh, Paul Newman's eyes?'

Joe's sunburnt face burned a deeper red.

Kazar twitched its limbs as if in a shrug. 'For your purposes, we shall call her Dijepa Coanman – or Jenny, for short.'

'Jenny,' Joe exhaled. 'Is she an alien?'

'At her core, yes. But you won't be seeing her core.'

Joe was seeing everything else, though, his eyes wandering over the wondrous woman's swollen breasts and jutting nipples, rappelling down her plump butt cheeks and along her lithe, golden legs, and then scaling back up her legs, resting briefly on her strip-shaved pussy before ascending to her globular tits again. He glanced quickly at her shining face and 'Friends'-era styled hair. He avoided her eyes.

'You will fuck her multiple times,' Kazar squeaked without compunction. Then he slithered into an opening at the bottom of the instrument panel, like a silverfish oozing under a refrigerator, leaving Joe and Jenny all alone together.

'Do you like what you see?' the celestial body spoke, eternity in her Kathleen Turner husky voice.

Joe hardened like an eight-foot length of green spruce in a fired kiln, the lumber visible in his tight jeans his universal response. He blessed the satellite dish back home, the space age technology that allowed him to watch all the shows and movies from which his best-of-the-best dream girl had been fashioned.

Jenny glided towards him, her tanned, toned body rippling and jiggling in all the right places. 'You were chosen because of your stamina, Joe, your ability to spill sperm early and often.'

Joe was honoured, horny as hell. He tore off his t-shirt and flung it aside, unlaced and kicked off his steel-capped boots, unbuckled and unzipped his faded blue jeans and shoved them down and off. Jenny looked at the man's very tighty-whities, and smiled.

She pushed her lush chest up against Joe's hairy trunk, and he grabbed on to her like a born-again tree-hugger, crushing her hot body against his. His cock pressed urgently into her flat belly, a sticky wetness already staining his underwear. She gazed up into his gaping, brown eyes and kissed him. He hungrily devoured her soft, moist, Angelina Jolie-like lips, and she gripped the sides of his Jockeys and yanked down.

After inflaming each other with their mouths and hands and sundry other body parts, Jenny fought her way out of Joe's hairy, blond arms and fell back onto a padded platform that had arisen as quickly and surely as the man's erection. 'Fuck me, Joe!' she hissed, spreading her slender legs and pulling her pink, Jenna Jameson, petals apart, urging him to dock his rocket.

47

Joe was on her like gravity on a Jovian. He pressed his bony, lanky body against her soft and cushiony one, his lips against her lips again, his sweaty hands rummaging around for her impossibly upright breasts and finding them. She slid a Gene Simmons tongue into his mouth and moaned like she meant it, Joe not-so-dry-humping her stomach.

'Fuck me, Joe!' she repeated.

He fumbled between his legs and grabbed hold of his cock and zipped its mushroomed hood right over her slit and into her Britney Spears bellybutton. It'd been awhile since he'd done this sort of bush work. She took his cock in her hand and pressed its boiled-up head into her juicy cunt, grabbed onto his pale buttocks and slammed him home.

'Yeah,' Joe mumbled, tonguing a Scarlett Johansson ear and pumping his hips in a rhythm as old as all creation.

Jenny gripped Joe's shoulders and urged him on with some Ginger Lynn dirty-talk. His thick cock sawed back and forth inside her with an oiled ease, faster and faster, until he was pounding her pussy with an animal intensity. Her Elvira-like fingernails bit into him, and he tilted his head back and howled at the moon, white-hot sperm launching from his balls and into her silky pink space.

'More! More!' she urged, as Joe shot his payload.

He collapsed on top of her, gasping for air, bathed in the sweat of his efforts (his first bath in quite some time).

'Fuck me up the ass, Joe,' she whispered in his ear, before pushing his deadweight away and doing a log-roll on the platform. She jumped up onto all-fours and wiggled her bold, bronze bum at him.

He responded like a bear to honey, possessing that rare ability of almost instant sexual recovery and semen rejuvenation. He reared up on his knees and trundled in behind her, steering his still-hard cock into her puckered, Nina Hartley asshole. His pole slid inside her like greased doweling, plunging right to the hairline. Then he gripped her Shakira hips and started banging away.

And only a minute or so after penetrating that taut, gripping bottom, watching those split-peach cheeks shudder resplendently as he smacked them repeatedly with his body, Joe went supernova a second time, shooting for the stars all over again. He tilted his head back and bellowed loud enough to register at the Arecibo Observatory, spraying sizzling spunk deep into Jenny's chute, into her core.

He toppled over on top of his out-of-this-world lover, sliding right off her sweat-dappled skin and landing with a thunk on the platform.

'More! Fuck me more!' she implored. She encircled his shaft with her Palmolive fingers and sealed her lips around his cap and sucked like a black hole.

They had hot star sex in every position imaginable, every Joe-brain-inspired orifice offered and explored. He leaked semen like his pick-up leaked oil. Until at last, when he was as spent as a white dwarf, Kazar reappeared. It squeaked at the woman to wake up the depleted, dozing woodsman, and she squirted milk into his face á la slut number four in Breastpumpers III, rousing Joe back to consciousness.

'Human, thank you for all your help,' Kazar shrilled.

Joe rolled off the platform and hit the floor pleading. 'No problem. I can do more,' he gasped. He staggered to his feet and stared at Jenny, picturing her with Eva Longoria's body for a change of pace.

'Unfortunately, you cannot stay long – and hard,' Kazar added with a smirk, 'in this atmosphere.' It gestured about the ship with a multitude of limbs. 'An atmosphere that allows the both of us to function. No man can. That's why we needed a man of your…special abilities, Joe. For to impregnate the one we call Jenny, much of your Earthly seed was required.'

'Impregnate!?' Joe yelped, coming back to his senses, his atrophied sense of responsibility.

Kazar grinned. 'Yes. I said this was the 'mother' ship, Joe. And thanks to you, Jenny can now give birth to another universe, just as she did fifteen billion of your years ago.'

Joe gave his head a shake, his penis now as shrivelled as little Kazar.

'You mean…I'm…'

'Yes, you're free to go.'

Fernie Brae
by Nyki Blatchley

She was sitting in the middle of a stone circle, when I first saw her. She sat cross-legged on the centre stone, watching me calmly. She was naked; but that was the least surprising thing about her. Though small and slim, she had a luscious figure, flared hips and conical breasts with sprawling aureoles. And her delicate complexion was of pale purple.

Her face was weirdly beautiful, long and thin with a snub-nose and full crimson lips, and her slanted eyes were golden. Pointed ears poked through waist-length hair that was a riot of red and blues, yellows and greens, and colours I couldn't quite name. And from her shoulders sprouted huge filigree wings.

I'd fallen asleep in the shadow of the standing stones, tired from a morning walking through the hills. I'd seen the tell-tale symbol on the map and planned my route to take it in. There are standing stones the length and breadth of Britain and beyond, many of them arranged in circles. They're magic places every one, with their mystical alignment to the heavens and their connection to the bones of the earth.

It would be worth the couple of extra miles, I'd thought, but had seriously begun to doubt it, as I'd slogged up the long path. No route is ever straight in the hills, but this one had twisted and wound more than most. Now, on the last stretch, the little track that might have been made by walkers, or might have been made by sheep, had wrapped itself round and round the hillside, spiralling in like a maze.

Even though in no real state to appreciate the sight, the circle had impressed me. A dozen worn pillars, erect and proud in an irregular ring, leaning like rotten teeth with a warm breeze playing through the gaps. Lichen grew on them, and one leant so far it seemed a miracle it hadn't fallen.

Inside the ring, the grass looked lusher than on the hilltop around. In the centre, a large flat stone was barely discernible above the waving green blades all around. Once I was within, all sound had seemed shut out, even the wind.

Slipping off my pack, I'd fished out my water-bottle and taken a long slug; then I'd lain down on my back in the grass, vaguely watching the sun flirting with wispy clouds. I'd only intended to close my eyes for a few minutes, but opened them to find the sun halfway down the sky and to the knowledge that I wasn't alone. I sat up abruptly.

'Who…' I managed before my voice ran out. The single word sounded loud in my ears, telling me that I wasn't dreaming.

She smiled. At least, it seemed like a smile, though her features were so strange that it was hard to be sure. 'Usually,' she said, 'I'm called *Your Majesty*.' She had a singing, lilting voice that sounded in harmony, partly from her mouth and partly from far away.

'Your…um…' It was reasonable enough to be tongue-tied in such a situation, but I felt acutely embarrassed to be mumbling in front of this exotic beauty. 'What's going on?' I managed at last.

'You've slept inside my Ring,' she said, the weird smile still playing with her lips and eyes. 'That makes you mine.'

'Your ring?' Glancing around, I realized that the standing stones no longer looked the same. To part of my sight, they were still stones, worn and lichen-covered; but they were also men, two or three times my own height and covered in shaggy hair. Their eyes were all fixed on the woman who spoke to me, and each had an erection as long as my forearm.

'My giant-guards,' she said. 'They watch over my sacred place, until I fuck each one of them. Then they'll be released.'

It was all so unreal that the thing which struck me most was that there was no crudity about the way her lilting voice said *fuck*. Instead, it seemed to come from a wonderful place, where music and sex were one.

'Are you a goddess?' I found myself asking. The question seemed absurd, but less absurd than what I was seeing with my own eyes.

But she laughed aloud, like bells in the wind. 'Not a goddess,' she said. 'Not one of those stuck-up, sanctimonious bitches.' Cocking her head on one side, she examined me. 'Don't you know me?' she challenged. 'I don't believe mortals have entirely forgotten me. I'm the Faery Queen.'

I didn't doubt her, in spite of the voice inside trying to tell me how stupid this was. I was speaking to a naked purple woman with wings, in the middle of standing

53

stones that were also giants. In what way was it reasonable to doubt who she was?

I was still sitting half up, leaning on my elbows. Before I could move further, I felt a slithering at my ankles. I glanced down, almost expecting to see snakes crawling all over me, but the grass was visibly growing around my feet, twining quickly and expertly to tie me down. In panic, I tried to pull my feet back; but, for all the apparent fragility of the grass, I was trapped by solid bonds.

Trying to sit up, I realized that there was more slithering where my arms rested, and they too were held tightly. Quickly and expertly, the grass wound up and around me, pulling me back to lie supine, winding itself around chest and waist and thighs. Before I'd managed to find words to protest, I was bound firmly to the ground.

'What's happening?' I finally managed.

Her strange face took on a surprised expression. 'What do you think?' she asked sweetly. 'There's only one use for mortals.'

Desperately racking my brains, I tried to remember what I knew of faery lore. I was vaguely familiar with the usual fairy-stories, of course, and I had half-memories of old ballads that seemed to deal with the subject a little more seriously. But, of course, I'd never regarded any of this as more than fanciful stories from long ago. How much of it was true? I wondered. Could I use the old tales as a guide?

'Are you going to kill me?' I asked her, struggling to keep a façade of calm that belied my actual feelings.

Her expression grew more unmistakably puzzled, and her head moved from side to side, almost like an animal searching for a scent. 'What's kill?' she asked. 'I think I may have heard of it once. But it's been so long.'

A little reassured, even though the weirdness was somehow increased, I said, 'It's to…make someone be dead.'

There was a long pause, this time. 'Oh, yes,' she murmured at last, the distant part of her voice sounding like a faint breeze, 'I remember death. I didn't like it, so I forgot about it.' The smile returned. 'Oh no,' she added, 'it's not death I want from you.'

I saw her make a slight movement with her hands, and realized instantly that my clothes had vanished. I still lay helpless in the bonds of the grass, but now I was naked.

'Ah,' she sighed, examining my body, 'mortal men are best. Women can be fun, but they haven't one of *these*.' And, kneeling forwards, she reached out one small, purple hand and brushed my flaccid penis.

Her touch was like nothing I'd ever felt before. The skin of her hand seemed to be both there and not there. It felt like cool velvet, with only the slightest of chafing to mark its passing; but it seemed to pass right through the organ as well, feeling it from the inside. It was a more intimate touch than any I'd ever felt, and I could feel the blood pulsing faster through my veins. She was very close to me, her purple skin sending a tingle through the air between us. I could see a sheen all over her, like and unlike sweat. It glittered golden in the sunlight, and smelled like rhododendrons after rain.

My mind was divided, like her voice and the stones. Part of it was watching and questioning, feeling scared. In spite of her assurance that she didn't want to kill me, I was being held captive for her pleasure, and was being whirled into sex. There was a panicky feeling, which I didn't entirely understand. I enjoyed sex; and the Faery Queen, strange as she might be, was certainly desirable. But I was used to feeling at least partly in control; and now the helplessness of my position felt like vertigo, sending me spinning and tumbling into chaos.

At the same time, though, my consciousness was crackling between her body and mine, and that cloyingly sweet smell seemed to have got into my blood. I could feel myself careering through my veins, waking the sleeping cells of a form that was more like light than flesh.

'This will be fun,' said the Faery Queen softly, and she began to leave tickling kisses on my body, something like a warm breeze on naked skin and something like the suction of two sweaty bodies pressed together. Her cool, barely-tangible lips explored every part of me, caressing with warm, musky breath that soaked into the pores of my skin. Her mouth lingered deliciously on my inner thighs and my nipples and the side of my neck and my own mouth.

A jag of light flashed across my eyes. The watching mind told me that, in a sky with few clouds, it couldn't be lightning; but then the rolling roar of thunder rose and fell, coming from every part of the sky at once. The lightning-fork had burnt itself into my sight, and I began to see two things at once, just as the stones were stones and giants, just as my captor's voice came from her lips and from far away. I could see the stone-circle, the Faery Queen looming over me with her lips to mine and her hand caressing my now responding penis; *and I could see a crossroads, with a narrow, unmade track climbing a steep hill to one side, a broad main road rolling gently downhill to the other, and a seductively winding country lane straight ahead, hung over with apple-blossom and lined by dog-roses, forget-me-nots and hawthorn.*

'What's happening?' I asked, when her mouth moved a little away from mine.

The Faery Queen's face took on that expression which might have been a smile. 'I'm going to take you,' she said softly, 'somewhere wonderful.' Sliding sinuously down my body, leaving trails of electricity buzzing beneath my skin, she took my half-erect member between thumb and forefinger and gently kissed its tip.

A sensation shot through my penis and deep into my belly, something like lightning and something like solid ice. I could feel her pulling the foreskin back over the head, a sweet little tongue-tip flickering at the slit. *But I couldn't concentrate, because I was standing at the crossroads too. The Faery Queen stood beside me, and I saw now that she was small, her head barely reaching my shoulder. But she was imperious, and the voice that came from far-off was telling me, 'This way, forget the other roads. This is the way we must go.'*

I heard her give a slight sigh before, pulling back her face a moment, she opened her crimson mouth wide and engulfed my erection in a single plunge. Leaving it there a moment, she drew her lips back, sliding them along topside and sensitive underside, until they'd reached the exposed knob, before swooping all the way back.

A shuddering passed all the way through my body, and I strained against my bonds, powerless to do anything else. It was like being tickled; but from within, deep inside my veins and my organs, deeper even than that. As though that mouth, damp and insistent, were kissing the inside of my soul. At the fullest plunge, her tongue tickled my balls and her teeth delicately combed through the tangled curls of my pubic hair. Then she would pull slowly back, her tongue-tip playing all the way up my undershaft, her lips following with a light, silky rasp, until she was teasing the head again.

After a few strokes, without losing rhythm, she moved around to straddle my face. Remembering how short she was, I doubted that she'd be able to continue her ministrations from that position; but her wet, open vagina planted its sweet kiss on my lips while her own mouth was at fullest plunge.

I'd always enjoyed the taste and smell of a woman's genitals, the rich, strong taste of the juices. But the Faery Queen was like no other woman. The aroma was like that from her pores, the lushness of the bloom that seduces the bee, but so wanton that my head spun with the scent. And she tasted sweet, like honey not sugar, with the delicate perfume of wildflowers. My tongue strained, without conscious effort, to drink in all it could of that heady liquor.

Deprived of sight and intoxicated by smell and taste, I found I was seeing the crossroads more clearly. 'Come with me,' she told me, and I'd no will to resist. Glancing to left and right, I felt no temptation to take the other roads. I briefly turned my head and saw that the road behind led, a very short distance away, to the stone circle where I lay naked, the Faery Queen astraddle my face and sucking on me.

'We'll catch up with ourselves,' she said, taking my hand in hers.

From somewhere in the air around me, a voice that might have been mine was singing a verse of an ancient ballad I remembered hearing once:

And see ye not yon bonny road
That winds around the fernie brae?
That is the Road to fair Elfland,
Where thou and I this night maun gae.

I looked at the exquisite creature beside me, so delicate and so commanding, and my heart missed a beat at the mere thought of not being with her. There was a hollow need in my guts, and a pounding in my chest, and a need in my mind; and I set off with her along the winding country lane.

As I walked, my tongue parted the little hood at the top of the Faery Queen's slit and freed the tiny knob of her clitoris. The moment I touched it, I felt her back arch and her mouth clamp tightly over my shaft for an instant, before she resumed her rhythm, and guessed that she had felt the icy lightning that she sent through my body.

I played for a while with the wonderful little thing, feeling it grow swollen and proud at the insistence of my tongue-tip, before I went exploring between her tightly-pursed lips, driven by a hunger to be inside her. I found the way in, by the sweet juices seeping from it, but it was hardly there.

I was scared to probe, thinking I'd hurt her; *but she turned to me as we wandered hand-in-hand around the windings of the country lane, pausing as two rabbits scampered across in front of us. 'Don't hold back,' she murmured, and her voice caressed me from within. 'On a road like this, nothing you do can harm me.'*

So I pushed my tongue into the tiny hole, feeling it open like tight elastic, squeezing back hard to prevent me from leaving, if I'd been mad enough to wish to. *'That feels good,' she giggled, her beautiful face sparkling into a smile. 'Lets run for a while.'*

Still hand-in-hand, we sprang into a fast run along the lane. Her filigree wings spread to catch the warm wind that blew her rainbow hair out behind; and the same wind played deliciously in my own hair and on my naked skin. The ground beneath my bare feet was springy grass now,

not warm tarmac, and I could feel the grass-roots growing
slowly through my soles and up through my blood-stream
to my heart. Exulting in speed and wind and life, I felt
myself spurting spasm after spasm of life into the Faery
Queen's open mouth.

'Oh no,' she said, lifting her head up from my soaked
penis, still pointing stiffly up but on the point of collapse.
'I haven't finished with this yet.' She passed her hand
lightly over it, and its erection became instantly solid
again, matching my undiminished desire.

'This road winds a lot,' I commented, *stopping for*
breath. I was feeling surprisingly good, after running so
far, but felt I needed a rest. 'I think it's turned right round
on itself.'

The Faery Queen regarded me with languid
amusement, stretching her wings luxuriously. *'Several*
times over,' she commented.

'So...' I glanced around, but nothing looked familiar.
'Why haven't we come back to where we started?'

'Because a circle doesn't do that,' she explained
patiently, reaching out to caress my hair. 'By the time a
circle can come back on itself, time has passed. So the new
circle begins from a different point.'

I considered, before deciding that this seemed
reasonable. *'So,'* I said, *'we keep going round and round,*
and always come to somewhere different?'

'Isn't that how you reach anywhere worth reaching?'

I didn't have a chance to reply, because she lifted her
beautiful buttocks off my eyes and her cute crotch off my
mouth and turned around in a single, fluid movement. Her
golden slanted eyes gazed down at me.

I longed to sit up, take her in my arms and lay her
down. I longed to lie over her and take her roughly,
feeling her delicate body helpless as I thrust into it. But the

grass bonds still held me tightly, and it was as much as I could do to raise my head.

With a sigh, the Faery Queen straddled my crotch, holding her wet, pink slit just over the object of its desire. 'I want this,' she said softly, 'inside me.'

I panicked for a moment, as she lowered herself slowly onto me, remembering how tiny the hole was and half-expecting to tear her apart. But it opened to accommodate the shaft, springing back to grasp it so tightly that I gasped, as the insistence of my surging blood fought with the velvet grip around it.

I stopped walking abruptly. 'I can hear someone singing,' I said.

'Of course. It's not far now.'

Whirling me by the hand she'd kept in mine, she grabbed my other hand and began a wild, capering dance, round and round. Her brilliant hair floated around her in ways that seemed to have little to do with her motion. Her pointy breasts were firmly aimed at me, their nipples, crimson against purple skin, erect and impossibly long. We whirled faster; and she was screaming, as she rose and fell on me, her flow-scent sweat dripping from her face and her breasts and her belly and her thighs, to merge shamelessly with the musky sweat of my passion. *We were whirling so fast that I could no longer see anything but her, as the land spun around us, and the wind was roaring in my head and on my skin, and my body was indistinguishable from hers or from the land we danced in;* and she reared up, her body liquid and shaking, her wings spread convulsively, as she sucked me right into herself and I poured spurt after spurt deep into her body.

I looked slowly around, as my head stopped its ecstatic spinning. 'How did I get here?' I asked dreamily.

The Faery Queen had her arms around me, her head nuzzling against my chest, wings half folded about us both. It didn't just seem natural to be like that, it would have seemed unnatural to be any other way. She didn't look, but I guessed that she knew what was there anyway.

'Don't you remember?' She gave a low throaty giggle. 'We came together.'

I couldn't disagree with that. The countryside around me glowed along every edge, gold and silver and a rainbow of colours. All the familiar objects, trees and grass, bushes and flowers, seemed both themselves and something totally other at the same time.

And there were people everywhere. Some were like the creature in my arms, winged and delicately coloured; others seemed to be beings out of myth, satyrs and nymphs, dwarves and giants. All were sexually engaged, in couple, threes or more, and in all combinations of male and female; though not all seemed restricted to the sexes I knew.

'Is this fairyland?' I asked at last.

'If that's what you want to call it,' she said. I wasn't sure whether her voice sounded annoyed or amused. 'It's my realm. You're welcome to make use of it.'

I looked around again, searching for the winding lane, but there was no sign of a road anywhere in this strange landscape. 'It would be nice for a while,' I said cautiously. 'But I've got a life, back at home.'

She gave a tinkling laugh that was suddenly no longer sweet. 'Not much of one, now. You've been gone seven years already.'

'What?' It wasn't the most eloquent reply, but it was all I could manage. 'How come?'

'Precisely,' she said. 'A faery fuck takes seven years: everyone knows that.'

I felt panic rising from my guts towards my throat and forced it down again. 'And...' I stuttered. 'And...how do I get back? The road's gone. Can you show me back?'

She threw back her head and laughed heartily this time. 'No, no, no,' she sang, more than spoke. 'My fuck shows the way here. There are others who show the way back.'

'Who?' I asked, glancing around. Though I wasn't happy about losing seven years, if the way back was as good as the way here, it might almost be worth it.

But the Faery Queen laughed again. 'I haven't the slightest idea,' she told me. 'You'll just have to try them all. But remember: seven years each time.'

My face must have looked horrified, because she giggled again and kissed me, deeply and sweetly, but not with passion. 'Come now,' she said, her voice a little more gentle, 'it's not so bad to be here, is it? You've pleased me, and my realm is yours to enjoy.'

At a sighing, tinkling call from her, two girls ran up, hand-in-hand. One was covered in silver fur, a long tail swishing behind, the other had hair of foliage and flowers for breasts. 'This is a visitor to our land,' she said. 'Make sure he enjoys himself.'

As they took my hands and pulled me after them, I shrugged inwardly. I still intended to get home, one day. But I'd have fun doing it.

Boob Hill
by Landon Dixon

John 'Long' Johnson held up a weather-browned hand, bringing to a halt the six horsemen and women trailing behind him. He pushed back his dusty, ten-gallon cowboy hat and shaded his brow, squinting stinging sweat out of his blazing blue eyes as he gazed down at the ramshackle collection of wood frame buildings and homes that were Dike City, Kansas. Shimmering waves of heat rose off the sun-baked land below, and the sluggish Little Snake River, which regularly overflowed its banks and the town's crudely constructed dykes, wound its way like a muddy artery through the burnt-stubble heart of the valley bowl.

'That her?' one of the men asked, bringing his mount alongside Johnson's.

'Yep,' was all the handsome, taciturn cocksman replied.

'Her' was a good description of the wind-whipped, bare-ass town, because Dike City, Kansas, was home to the infamous Boob Hill – a barely-legal brothel that was busy turning the local female population into howling nymphomaniacs. Married men were being left wifeless, families daughterless, single men ecstatic by the depraved goings-on at the sprawling whorehouse. Good-hearted, god-fearing womenfolk would enter the brothel on a mission of mercy and never leave, turned on to the powerful pleasures of the flesh by the devious Madam of the house, Lurlene 'Chesty' Laflemme.

By hypnosis or potion, or some other means unknown, Chesty would transform the modest little ladies of the prairies into sex-craved she-devils that no one man could ever hope to satisfy. The reborn brazen babes needed, craved, men, and plenty o' 'em, and Chesty provided the man-meat to temporarily satiate their overwhelming hunger, at a tidy profit to herself, of course.

Johnson had been hired by the town council, twelve married men good and true, to put a stop to it – to tame Chesty and lift the gate on her ever-expanding corral of lust-addled women, to reunite families torn asunder by all-consuming carnality. Sure, the single men, and a good many of the married, too, had objected to the Town hiring Johnson, but most of those men weren't landowners, and, thus, couldn't vote, so their opinions counted as much as cow chips to the political leaders who felt the Wild West had no place in Dike City.

'We gonna hit her tonight?' another of Johnson's mob inquired.

'Naw,' the well-endowed tail boss drawled. 'We'll hit 'er come mornin', when the debauchery's at low ebb.'

The attractive group of cowboys and girls nodded, confident of Johnson's skills on the range, the battlefield, and in the sack. Every clam-shaped notch on Johnson's rifle stock spoke of his abilities of seduction and survival. There were a hundred and twenty-five such notches in all.

Johnson kicked a glowing ember back into the campfire, then squatted down and tilted a tin cup of hot, black coffee up to his thick, sensuous lips, taking a good, long draught.

Somewhere far off in the night-shaded wilderness frisky coyotes barked love songs back and forth, while lusty gophers made chattering love in their funk-smelling burrows. Good signs, all.

Johnson sagely regarded the flame-licked faces of his posse, liked what he saw: three men – experienced, dick-heavy dudes who could cunny-ride the orneriest of ladies; and three women – big-breasted beauts who kept their men's tools well-oiled, and pacified any stray males who got in their way.

'Mebbe y'all should work on your moves some, so y'all be ready come mornin',' Johnson instructed.

The sex-hardened gang quickly jumped to their feet and shucked their buckskin like it was crawling with fire ants. They stood nude and lewd before the flickering campfire, the men's iron-hard dongs bobbing long and heavy and sure, cocked for action, the women's hefty, heaving jugs swollen with mother's milk, begging to be sucked dry. Then they paired off, started getting down and dirty with each other.

Johnson studied their technique, mindful of any flaws that could get a man bucked, a woman chucked. He drew his own ten-inch cum-cannon out of its cotton holster and commenced to stroking, watching Lynn 'Man-Eater' Craven tease Cal 'Sure-Shot' McGroot's lengthy prod with her playful, pink snake of a tongue. Her awesome, snow-white tits, capped by inch-long, rosy-red nipples, swayed ponderously from side to side as she licked all over Cal's hard wood. Then she ably swallowed the groaning man's timber in one slobbery gulp, her fiery-red hair cascading across her pretty face.

Lynn bobbed her head up and down on the bucking cowboy's bushwhacker, sucking hard and sure with precision mouth-strokes, from bloated tip to furry base, till she finally yanked Cal's dripping lady-killer out of her stretched-wide mouth and asked, 'Y'all gonna fuck my titties, or what?'

Johnson's lips creased into a smile, as he pulled on his pecker with a calloused, practiced hand, looking on appreciatively as Lynn cupped and seductively juggled her over-ripe melons. Her magnificent, blue-veined mams were enough to tempt even a not-so-straight-shooter to bury his spunk-gun in between her soft mountains and lighten his load, frost her flesh-cones.

Cal ambled closer and eased his throbbing rod into Lynn's heated chest canyon, began churning his hips in a dosey-do as old as the Jism Trail itself. Lynn shoved her ivory mounds together, smothering Cal's pumping dong, then spat into her tit-tunnel to grease the action even further. Cal sawed his saddle horn back and forth in the redhead's depthless cleavage, fucking her treasure chest faster and faster, pinching and rolling her fully-flowered nipples as best he could. And Lynn stuck out her tongue, providing a warm, wet cushion for Cal's peek-a-booing cocktop.

Cal rode roughshod over Lynn's tremulous titties, blazing a heated, humid, velvety path between her jouncing jugs, till he broke the flesh-spanked night air open with a yowl of satisfaction and blasted a bandolierful of white-hot jizz onto the girl's all-natural endowment. He coated Lynn's neck, her cupped casabas, with the unerring accuracy of a man who'd corralled and domesticated a passel of damsels in distress (and out of 'dis dress'). Lynn joyously rubbed Cal's salty jerk into her massive, shiny breasts, revelling in her own wicked powers of tit-suasion.

Johnson's shrewd eyes roamed over the rest of his merry, messy band of fucking and sucking cummers, confident that they could handle the wayward women of

Boob Hill. He tucked his own purple-knobbed fuck-stick back into his trousers, saving his juice for the personal challenge that lay ahead – a high-poon showdown with the dangerous, money and man-lusting proprietress of Boob Hill, Chesty Laflemme.

Come the crack of dawn, Johnson rose up on his hind legs and stretched, felt his manhood to ensure it was in working order, and then roused the rest of his posse. The plan was simple: take on all comers, cum on all takers – hands-on demonstrate to the horny, horn-swoggled women of Boob Hill that one man could, indeed, satisfy one woman, and then return the satiated gals to their rightful families.

The group of well-hung twat-tamers and their busty cock wranglers mounted up, cantered off the high ground and down towards Dike City, rocking sensuously back and forth in their polished leather saddles. They were trotting Main Street in a matter of a minutes, then pulled up and looked towards the end of the deserted street, where on a rocky, barren plateau stood the gaily-lit brothel that would be the sexy scene of Johnson and his gang's showdown/ho-down with Laflemme and her lusty ladies of the evening, and morning, and afternoon.

The gang dismounted, and with the torpedo-titted women covering their broad backs, the thick-membered men trod the dirty, grey planks of the sagging wooden sidewalk, resolutely striding past shuttered storefronts and up the hill to the den of iniquity that had laid claim to so many normally monogamous women. The brothel was a gaudy, rambling mansion of twenty-some rooms, as structurally unappealing as a temperance tomboy with bumps where breasts should've grown. Johnson didn't waste time skinning his knuckles on the red-painted front door; instead, a well-placed boot splintered the entryway and his posse passed inside.

They crossed a long, marble entrance hall, climbed a spiralling, red-carpeted staircase, and then trundled down an upstairs corridor. Johnson fanned his men and women out in front of him, and they burst open doors and leaped into chambers framed in chiffon and doused in perfume, taking the slumbering, all-too-temporarily satiated women of the house of ill-repute unawares. The heavy-breasted cowgirls pulled the paying customers aside, using their ample charms to convince the stunned johns to make love, not war, while the three-legged cowboys bared their loins and put into practice their studly powers of seduction, rustling up memories in the confused ladies' minds of just how sweet and sweaty it was to be a one-man woman.

Johnson, meanwhile, moseyed off further down the hall, in search of even breastier babes to stamp with his brand. When he reached the end of the long, wallpapered passage, he toed the last door in line open and strode inside, found one Lurlene 'Chesty' Laflemme ensconced in the bubbly chop of a cast-iron bathtub like a siren in the sea. Johnson could tell it was she, both from the fact that her striking face matched the Wanted poster he carried on his person, and the fact that, even though her body was completely submerged in the soapy water, her Sierra Nevada-like breasts still peeked their pink tips out of the suds.

'Been lookin' for ya, Chesty,' Johnson drawled, slowly and carefully unbuttoning his buckskin jacket.

'Been waitin', long rider,' Chesty replied, a defiant smile lifting the corners of her crimson lips. Her sun-bleached, blonde hair was piled atop her head like a stook of ripened wheat, with a blood-red rose stuck in its midst, thorns and all. She pushed her mams still further out of the bursting bubbles, till they glistened huge and hypnotic in the oil-lamp light, gargantuan in size, tanned an almost all-over tawny, saddle leather brown and twin-peaked by jutting nipples that looked like they could spray enough white gold to satisfy the most parched of '49ers.

'What's it all about, big 'uns?' Johnson asked, cautiously dropping his jacket, going to work on his flannel shirt, warily avoiding any sudden movements that might spook the big, brazen, bathing mama. 'Why you turnin' good women bad, wives into wantons?' Chesty regarded him steadily with her slate-grey eyes, watching as the loaded-for-bare cunt rustler deftly unbuttoned his shirt, shunted it aside. She surveyed Johnson's hairy, muscular chest and licked her bee-stung lips. 'A girl's gotta have her gold,' she replied. 'And business is boomin', big man.'

'That the only reason?' Johnson inquired, well-knowing that dollars and cents weren't the only factors at play here. The weaker sex coveted coin and carnal knowledge as much as the male of the species, sure, but they coveted something else even more, something that all the money in the world couldn't buy – love, sweet, love.

Chesty blushed, looked down, up, at her tremendous, sud-sprinkled titties. 'I was a one-man woman once,' she spoke softly. 'But then he ran away with a two-bit bar floozy and...' She glanced angrily up at Johnson, whose pants were now down around his ankles, his rigid dick sticking out like a flagpole at a frontier fort, waiting to be saluted. 'Well, let's just say that I vowed to never let that happen again, and filthy lucre became my one true love; you treat it well and it'll never leave you.'

'Money's cold comfort on a long winter's night – 'specially 'round these parts,' Johnson stated.

'I've plenty of one-night stands to keep my bones warm through the winter months,' Chesty responded. 'So don't think for a damn minute that you can bring me back in line with that handsome pussy-prod of yours, cunt-puncher,' she sneered, her spongy, soap-lathered boobs undulating as she slid upright in the bath, her glittering eyes locked on Johnson's twitching trenching tool.

'Well, ma'am, we'll just have to see about that,' Johnson said modestly, lifting his snakeskin cowboy boots out of his puddled denim trousers. He stood before the dripping, over-endowed frontier goddess, the both of them as naked as Adam and Eve save for the ten-gallon hat and size-fourteen pair of boots Johnson was wearing. And then he rushed her.

Chesty toppled the tub over on its side and spilled out of the bathwater, was on her bare feet in the blink of a third eye, brandishing a steely eighteen-inch dildo in her clenched right fist.

Johnson slid to a stop on the slickened floor and held up his hands. 'Whoa there now! You put that hole-plugger down, ma'am,' he intoned.

'This is all the man I need!' Chesty shrieked. 'Maybe you wanna try it on for size yourself!?' She hurtled herself at Johnson, the metallic cock-substitute aimed ass-high.

Johnson scrambled backwards, slipped, and crashed to the floor. He desperately kicked out his right boot, caught Chesty's shin, and knocked the top-heavy madam off her feet. She cried out in alarm, flailed her arms, and then landed smack dab on top of Johnson's propped-up pecker. Her sticky, splayed pussy lips caught on the cowboy's bloated dickcap, and then her downward momentum buried his massive schlong to the hairy balls inside her stretched-out pink.

Johnson pinned Chesty's arms to her side and frantically pumped his hips, savagely fucking the discombobulated babe before she even knew what hit her. Her foot-and-a-half-long lady-pleaser/man-smasher lay on the wet floor, as defunct now as the twin cities of Sodom and Gomorrah.

Johnson pounded the tittified gal's poon with his prong, fucking her relentlessly, striving to pacify her, to demonstrate beyond any reasonable doubt that one man could readily satisfy one woman, even a huge-breasted, jilted woman. And when Chesty finally let out a soft sigh of surrender, Johnson knew he was hitting his mark. He released her arms and grabbed up her overhanging jugs, fondled and squeezed her sodden, stunning breastworks.

Chesty closed her eyes and moaned, dug scarlet fingernails into Johnson's striated chest, pumping her firm, round bottom in rhythm to his urgent thrusting. Johnson knew then that he'd at last brought law and the natural order of things back to Dike City, Kansas. He rolled Chesty's rock-hard, distended nipples between his long fingers, kneaded her smooth, sun-kissed, Texas-sized titties, the muscles on his arms standing out in stark relief as he feverishly worked tit and banged twat.

The pace of the Westerners' frenetic coupling grew even more intense, and the chest-blessed gal bleated in ecstasy and Johnson grunted with satisfaction at a job well done. He blasted wad after wad of heavy-calibre cum deep into Chesty's gushing gash. Steaming justice had been served.

The Boob Hill brothel now sits as empty as a politician's promise, abandoned by its proprietress and her minions of man-lust, the wives returned to their loving husbands, the daughters to the warm bosoms of their families. The Johnson posse disbanded shortly after the graphic action at Boob Hill, the Wild West, it was clear to see, becoming a whole lot less wild. And Lurlene 'Chesty' Laflemme and John 'Long' Johnson? Well, they bought a spread due south of Dike City and hung up their guns, hers in a bra, his in a clean pair of hand-spun drawers, for hire no longer.

Serving Girls
by Teresa Joseph

It was only supposed to be a part-time cleaning job, a bit of extra money to help pay off the credit card bills. After all, it was common knowledge in the town where I lived that Mrs Simmons was always looking for maids, cleaners and other staff to help run her massive hilltop mansion. But as you've probably guessed from the fact that I'm taking the time to write this story, from the moment that I arrived for my interview I could never have imagined what would happen next, and I'm still not quite sure if it did.

Of course, if I'd even *suspected* that Mrs Simmons was engaged in anything untoward then I never would have applied for the job in the first place. But then again, I suppose that the best kept secret is one that everyone knows about but that nobody ever mentions, meaning that I probably just happened to apply for the job a few weeks before the rumours filtered down to my level.

Even if I had been aware of the gossip however, I probably would have laughed it off as an exaggerated joke. After all, Mrs Simmons looked about as dangerous and subversive as a plastic Barbie Doll, an impression that was probably helped by the fact that the plastic '*Dream*

House' lifestyle was the one thing that she had spent her whole life trying to emulate.

A tall, slim and beautiful blonde in her early forties, Janet Simmons had married for money at the age of seventeen and been widowed at the age of twenty-six, inheriting a hilltop mansion, two yachts and a fleet of cars which, as a telling statement of things to come, she immediately painted bright baby pink.

Every item of clothing, every pair of stilettos, every lipstick, and every bottle of nail varnish, everything that she owned was either white or baby pink. But while anyone else would have been considered insane, since she was a millionaire who was desperate to spend every penny of her fortune, Mrs Simmons was merely *eccentric* and we were all more than happy to help her achieve her goals.

It was common knowledge that, if you wanted to work for Mrs Simmons, it really helped your application if you happened to fit her mental image of a perfect living doll. And so, ironically, for the first time in my life, being tall and very slim with long red hair and legs to die for turned out to be a serious problem, even though I didn't realize it until it was far too late.

Whether you were a potential pin-up girl or not however, the cardinal rule for anyone who wanted to work for Mrs Simmons was that you *had* to play along with her 'Barbie Girl' delusions. And so in my naivety, thinking that it was nothing more than a harmless role-playing fantasy, on the day of my interview I dolled myself up with bright pink blusher, lipstick and nail varnish, wore my skimpiest and sexiest white T shirt, pink mini-skirt and strappy white stilettos. And from the moment that I parked my car, walked up to the main gate and buzzed the mansion's intercom, I beamed inanely from ear to ear and emptied my head of every meaningful thought.

'Hello?' Asked Mrs Simmons in her usual sickly sweet tone of voice.

'Hello, Mrs Simmons.' I beamed, perfecting the role of the air-headed bimbo before I'd even been allowed in the front door. 'My name is Lucy. I'd like to come and work for you, and so you said that I should come and see you today.'

It was really difficult for me not to use the words '*appointment*' or '*interview*'. But then again, Barbie dolls aren't supposed to use such long and complicated words.

'Come in then, darling,' she invited warmly as the main gates swung open to allow me inside. 'I'll ask one of my maids to let you in as soon as you arrive.'

Not wanting to upset my future employer with the sight of anything that wasn't pink, I left my Peugeot parked outside and walked up the main driveway towards the house as seductively as possible, past more than half a dozen sexy female gardeners who were also dressed in baby pink mini-skirts and grinning from ear to ear.

'Hello, madam,' beamed the sexy Asian maid who answered the front door in the same 'Stepford Wife' manner. 'Mrs Simmons is waiting for you. Please follow me.'

I never did learn the woman's name, but as I followed her through the marble-clad reception hall and up the main flight of stairs, I couldn't help but notice the fact that she looked more like a strip-o-gram than a normal domestic maid.

Leaving aside the fact that she was sexier than I was with a gorgeous dark complexion, long 'shampoo advert' hair, a perfect hourglass figure and legs that most women would kill for, her skimpy pink uniform was so kinky and erotic that it almost made *me* want to fuck her.

It was the most perfectly tailored piece of smut that I've ever seen in my life. And despite being completely strapless, it still managed to present her gorgeous cleavage for the whole world to see, while at the same time leaving her delectable back and shoulders on display.

Her skirt too, such as it was, was as short and skimpy as anyone could ever have gotten away with, puffed up with layer upon layer of lacy white petticoats that left even more of her legs, rump and pussy on display.

As I followed her up the long marble staircase, I couldn't help but be amazed at how elegantly she was able to walk in her 5" baby pink stiletto heels. But of course, having taken the time to appreciate the bows of her white satin stocking and suspenders and the intricate embroidery of her petticoats, it wasn't long before the only thing that I could think about was her smooth, naked pussy.

I think that this was my first real moment of doubt and panic. What if all of Mrs Simmons's domestic staff was required to dress like this? What if she was a total pervert?

Looking back on it now, of course, I suppose it's easy to say that I should have just turned around and walked back to my car without another word. But while I know that if my future employer had been a man then I would have run screaming to the nearest police station, the very fact that Mrs Simmons was a woman left me so confused that I didn't know what to do.

'She doesn't *look* like a dyke,' I thought to myself, just proving how naïve, ignorant and prejudiced I really was.

I just simply couldn't conceive of the possibility that a woman who was obsessed with the Barbie doll lifestyle could be a lesbian. And so because I couldn't understand it, I simply pushed it to the back of my mind and pretended that it didn't exist.

'Mrs Simmons, your guest is here,' announced the maid as she showed me through to her mistress's parlour.

'Thank you, darling,' she said dismissively. 'You can go now.'

Despite the lateness of the hour and her perfect make-up and hair, like every good playgirl living in the lap of luxury, Mrs Simmons was dressed in a beautifully tailored satin corset and fur lined gown with furry pink stiletto-heeled slippers and white silk stockings and suspenders, all of which seemed to have been deliberately chosen for their erotic sensuality. And as she lay there seductively, casually displaying the tops of her thighs and her huge ripe cleavage, I did actually wonder if I had accidentally walked into a 'Playboy' photo shoot.

Sprawling decadently across her plush pink velvet sofa as she sipped her champagne and nibbled her Belgian chocolates, it was fully five minutes before Mrs Simmons even acknowledged my existence. And since I was still too busy trying to figure out if I should be trying to impress her or running for my life, I just stood there like a mindless mannequin and smiled like a good little doll.

As it turned out of course, this was the best, or possibly the worst, thing that I could have done, because even though I didn't realize it, the interview had already begun.

Mrs Simmons wanted all of her staff to be as patient as a saint, willing to stand seductive and motionless for hours on end without ever breathing a single word. And so when the woman did finally stand to greet me, she was *very* pleased indeed.

'Hello, Lucy,' beamed the woman as she walked up to me and gave me a long, intimate hug, putting her cheek to mine and kissing the air to avoid smudging her lipstick. 'I'm sorry to have kept you waiting.'

'That's alright, Mrs Simmons.' I smiled in assent. 'I don't mind at all.'

Once I'd said that however, I quickly realized that I'd burned my bridges behind me and committed myself to taking the job. Because while it might sound completely insane, now that I'd said that I wanted to be there, I felt that it would be rude of me to refuse her or to try and leave.

'Very pretty,' she complimented in a smooth, seductive tone of voice as she lovingly examined my pert round breasts and slipped her hand up my skirt. 'I see that you've shaved your pussy for me. Yes, very nice indeed.'

By this point of course, all doubt and uncertainty had left my mind. Every fibre in my body was screaming at me to turn around and run back to the car as fast as I possibly could. But as Mrs Simmons leaned forward to give me a long, loving kiss on the lips, even though I wanted to stop her, I quickly realized that I was behaving more obediently than ever before.

It was as if my body was on auto-pilot. And while I wanted to shout at the woman to leave me alone, when I opened my mouth to yell at her, I heard myself say something completely different.

'Thank you, Mrs Simmons,' I beamed as she continued to compliment the smoothness of my pussy, even spreading my legs a little further apart to facilitate her inspection. 'I think that you're very pretty as well.'

I wanted to breathe a sigh of relief when Mrs Simmons finally turned to head back to her sofa. But instead, I actually heard myself whimper with frustration when the groping stopped. And while the second part of my interview wasn't quite as invasive as the first part had been, it was still so humiliating that I literally wanted to die.

Even though I couldn't make myself leave, as Mrs Simmons offered me a seat and began asking all sorts of embarrassing questions, I'm certain that I should have at least turned bright red with embarrassment. But as I sat down in the most lady-like fashion imaginable, still grinning from ear to ear and fluttering my eyelashes like an obedient bit of fluff, I didn't even feel myself become flushed.

'So, do you like licking pussy?' she smiled, as casually as if she were asking me about the weather.

'Yes, madam. Yes I do,' I beamed in reply. 'I'm a good little girl and I'll do whatever I'm told.'

What the hell was happening to me? I might have taken part in the odd '*experiment*' when I was at school, but I certainly wasn't a lesbian. And even if I was, why would I be talking about licking pussy in front of a woman who I'd only just met?

'And would you like to lick my pussy?'

'Oh yes, madam,' I panted, going down on all fours and crawling up to the woman as she playfully uncrossed her legs. 'Please let me lick your pussy. I'm such a good little girl.'

If I'd been watching someone else demean themselves in such a humiliating manner I would have either stormed out in total disgust or simply closed my eyes and turned away. But as she revealed her smooth naked pussy, petting my head as if I was one of her pets as she lovingly guided my lips towards her slit, there was nothing I could do to stop myself as I felt my mouth begin to water with eager anticipation and my pussy became just as wet.

'That's it, darling,' she purred as patronizingly as could be, licking her lips with satisfaction as I greedily lapped at her smooth wet slit. 'You lick Mummy's pussy like a good little girl.'

There was nothing that I could do to stop myself as I greedily buried my tongue inside her and licked and sucked as deeply as I could. I was even frigging the crotch of my white cotton panties so hard that I was actually starting to enjoy it.

No matter what it was that Mrs Simmons had done to turn me into an obedient lesbian puppet, she now had undeniable proof that it had worked perfectly. And now that she knew there was no chance of me being able to break her hold over me and escaping to tell other people what I had seen, she finally decided to '*offer me the job*'.

'Thank you darling, that's enough.' She smiled, gently easing my mouth away from her pussy and slowly re-crossing her legs.

Once again it seemed that while I was glad to see the end of my humiliation, my body was still as eager as ever. And as I watched Mrs Simmons ring the tiny ornamental 'service' bell on the table beside her seat, I actually remember wagging my bottom like a horny puppy and grinning from ear to ear with her honey glistening on my lips.

Mrs Simmons did ask me to stand back up before her maids arrived, of course, and I obeyed at once like a good little toy. But as two of the woman's other mindless playthings entered the room and their mistress gave them their instructions, I quickly realized that my humiliation was just beginning.

'Mary, Janet, this is Lucy,' she introduced us graciously, her pussy still tingling with orgasm after the licking that I had given her. 'Say hello, girls.'

'Hello Mary. Hello Janet.' I waved, beaming moronically like a character off Playschool.

'Hello Lucy.' They waved just as ridiculously in reply.

A tall stunning blonde and a brunette, dressed in the same skimpy pink French maid uniform that I'd seen before, the women were both incredibly beautiful and sexy. And thanks to Mrs Simmons's control over me, the very sight of them made my pussy tingle more than ever.

'Lucy wants to work for me, just like you do,' explained the woman as her two French maids came over to touch, caress and compliment my body, cooing with delight as if I were a cute little puppy. 'Please make her all pretty and teach her everything that she needs to know.'

'Yes, Mrs Simmons,' they curtsied. And the next thing I knew, I was being hurried out of the room and downstairs to the servants' quarters, ready to be bathed, powdered and dressed up in pink, ready to serve my pretty new mistress.

'Does that feel good?' cooed Janet, having stripped me naked and helped me into a hot, delightful bubble bath, paying particular attention to my breasts and pussy.

Whether it was how Mrs Simmons had programmed them or not, the look of sexual lust on the pretty maid's face as she eagerly lathered up my firm tanned breasts was absolutely undeniable. And of course, if I'd had a mirror, then I probably would have seen the same look on my own face as well.

Having stood me up and dried me off with towels so fluffy that they actually made me giggle, Mary and Janet then gently applied soft white talcum powder all over my body with huge fluffy powder puffs before wrapping me up in a soft pink bath robe and sitting me down to receive my full makeover.

As the sexy Asian maid expertly removed the varnish from my toenails and gave me the most relaxing pedicure of my life, Janet did the same to my fingers and Mary washed and styled my hair.

I suppose that since Mrs Simmons spent almost half her live being pampered in this manner; it was only natural that her domestic staff would be expert beauty therapists. And I must say that once Mary had removed my make-up, moisturised my skin and made my face up once again, I was absolutely astonished by the result.

'Are you a pretty little dolly now?'

The maid giggled as she put away her make-up and brushes.

'Oh yes,' I gasped unable to look away from my beautiful reflection or get over how wonderful I felt. 'I'm a *very* pretty dolly indeed.'

'Well, now it's time for us to dress you in your uniform,' she squealed as she clapped her hands together with glee. And five minutes later, I was gasping with delight as I felt the soft silk and satin uniform and stockings gently caress my skin.

I was a maid, I was a dolly, and I was also one of the girls. And as Mary and Janet playfully instructed me in all of the skills and nuances that I would have to master, I actually felt myself become so happy and horny that I actually *wanted* to be Mrs Simmons's sweet little plaything more than anything else in the world.

Tottering around the mansion in my 5" stiletto heels like a typical *Ooh la la* French maid in a 'Carry On' film, I got such a perverted sexual thrill from tickling around Mrs Simmons furniture and nick-nacks with my fluffy pink feather duster that my pussy simply would not stop dripping. And when Mrs Simmons came to praise my hard work and offered to reward me with a nice long lick of her pussy, I was so horny and eager to please her that I literally fell down onto my knees and hungrily worshipped her gorgeous slit.

'Do you like your new job then?' asked my new goddess as I desperately frigged my hot wet cunt, eagerly licking her glorious pussy as the honey began to pour down my chin.

'Oh yes, madam!' I panted, stopping as briefly as I could for a gasp of air before eagerly burying my tongue inside her once again. 'I love being your pretty little dolly! Please let me be your maid for ever!'

'Hush, darling, don't worry about a thing,' she said in an increasingly sexy but ominous tone of voice. 'I'll never send you away or ask you to leave. After all, I've got a lot of plans for you.'

Evelyn
by Courtney Bee

The first thing he felt was the burning, the rawness, where the ropes bit into his wrists and ankles. Next was the throbbing. Though he was lying stiffly on his back, limbs pulled taut, he felt as if he were riding a roller-coaster, his head reeling. When his eyes fluttered open, a blur of shapes and colours stung his corneas, and it took several minutes before his vision sharpened enough to distinguish objects.

His eyes darted around the room. When he saw the *Double Indemnity* poster, there was a spark in his brain. An apartment. Her apartment. But what was *her* name? He couldn't remember. He combed his memory, struggling to put the pieces of the evening together. He had gone to the Rumba Room – that much he remembered. The music had been loud, the walls were pulsating. Then he had spotted her. She was sipping an apple martini at the bar, her raven hair seizing the light like obsidian, shining from across the room. He couldn't say why, but he knew before she turned her head that she would be breathtaking, and his breath caught in his throat as she slowly looked over her shoulder, her gaze fixed on him like a laser. They glittered like diamonds, her eyes, and he was startled to find them an electric shade of violet, so intense that he faltered backward. She had skin pale as milk, a striking contrast to the full, berry-coloured lips that curved into a knowing smile. Her dress was black as the shadows surrounding her, wrapping around her like a velvet serpent. She was of another era, her look too ethereal to be a Miami native. European, perhaps?

Before he could think he felt his feet carrying him toward her, parting the throngs of tanned dancers and making his way to the smiling beauty. When he stood before her, a hint of her perfume curled around his nostrils, a scent surprisingly sweet, like ripe fruit.

'I – I thought I'd have something witty to say by the time I made it over here,' he said. 'Will you settle for shy and flustered?'

Her eyes were warm. 'Sounds endearing.'

She sipped her drink, taking long, languid sips.

'What's your name, shy and flustered?'

'Oh – it's Adam. Adam Belmont.'

She tilted her head and laughed a laugh that was light in sound but rich with wickedness.

'What's so funny?'

She brushed a long, dark tendril from her face and tucked it behind her ear.

'I'll tell you later,' she said. She set down the drink. 'Perhaps at my apartment?'

'I...'

Her smile widened. 'Yes?'

'I wasn't trying to get you into bed,' he said quickly. 'Well, maybe at some point, but I swear I didn't come over here to imply that tonight I wanted –'

'Take it easy, shy and flustered.'

She was studying him, her eyes sparkling with interest as they roamed his damp palms, his flushed cheeks, the way he bit his lower lip ever so subtly, chewing out his nervousness.

'I know you weren't implying anything,' she said. 'Perhaps you wanted to chat for a while, talk about the humidity or something of that nature? That's perfectly fine. But allow me to be blatant: my apartment is nearby, I've had several Red Bulls, and my legs are parting as we speak.'

Adam's jaw fell open, eliciting another laugh from the woman. He compelled his mouth to move, to form words, to stop stuttering like an idiot. She rose from her seat, bridging the gap between them. Her eyes burned into his, letting him know that there was only one answer she would deem acceptable.

'I've never had a one night stand,' he said, then quickly added, 'not that I want it to be just a one night stand.'

'Well, then,' she whispered. 'Make my toes curl tonight and you'll be invited back.'

She leaned close. He could smell the sweetness of her breath; such an unusually tart scent. It made him think of strawberries, apples, juicy plums. He could practically taste her.

'Shall we go now, Adam?'

He nodded so hard that he felt as if his head were about to unhinge itself from his neck. Her slender fingers curled around his palm, towing him gently toward the door. He followed like a puppy.

'I'm Evelyn, by the way.'

The evening air bit their flesh in a refreshing wave, the breeze tinged with the smell of ocean. As the door slammed shut behind them and they moved silently through the night, the music became a dull thump in the distance. The massive palm trees lining the streets were lit with strands of flickering lights, making shadows stretch and curl around them.

Adam had been at a loss of words before, but he now found himself petrified as the woman pointed to a building several blocks away.

'That's it,' she said. 'Didn't I tell you it was close?'

Adam nodded. He turned his head to look at her and was surprised to find that her expression was blissful, as if being outside in the darkness soothed her from the inside out. Actually, it was only when the silver wisps of clouds spread like a spider web across the moon and the stars struggled to be heard in the bleakness of the midnight sky that she felt truly at peace. But to Adam she merely appeared to be relieved to be out of the stifling, sweat-drenched club.

A tall Spanish-style building greeted them at the end of their journey, a dimly lit sign reading 'Garden East' apartments, announcing its purpose. Vines of bright red flowers hugged the building from every angle, springing from the lush garden surrounding the apartments. A little slice of paradise on an otherwise unremarkable street.

She led him up a flight of stairs, twisted her key into the lock, and flicked on the lights. Her apartment glistened with intellect and refinement. Paintings of exotic settings, stacks of leather-bound books, and intricately carved furniture that looked as if it had been plucked right from the rococo period. The *New York Times* on the kitchen table was the final item that convinced Adam that he wasn't about to have sex with a promiscuous bimbo. After surveying her elegant apartment, his fascination with the woman had doubled.

Evelyn breezed behind him, glided to the kitchen, and fetched two glasses, which she promptly filled with a ruby liquid from an unmarked bottle.

'You seem a bit nervous,' she smiled, handing him a glass. 'Try this. It's a lovely wine from Europe. My favourite, actually.'

He stared hesitantly at the glass. 'I don't know – I've had a few gin and tonics as it is. Maybe I shouldn't...'

She leaned close and met his gaze. Her eyes were glowing amethyst, burning with insistence.

'You must try it,' she said. 'It's a very special wine. I opened it because, well...you seem like a very special guy.'

He felt himself blush and tightened his grip around the drink.

'I don't know if I should...'

She raised her glass high above her mouth and tilted it slightly, until a single crimson droplet fell onto her lips, coating them in wetness. She licked up the moisture with her tongue, slowly, methodically, moaning with pleasure as the taste of it flooded her mouth.

Her eyes locked on his. 'You really...must...try it.'

He brought the wine to his mouth and urged it down his throat. He felt himself sigh, surprised by its richness.

'Wow,' he marvelled, wiping his lips. 'If wine were candy, this would definitely be dark chocolate.'

She seemed pleased and ushered him into the living room.

'Please, have a seat.'

Adam sank into the plush sofa. The woman sat beside him, flashing him an encouraging smile. His eyes fell to the *Double Indemnity* poster near the mantle, framed in an ornate gold casing.

'I remember that movie,' he said. 'It scared me when I was little – the chick, I mean. Femme fatale – is that what they're called? Scared me to death. The thought of someone actually planning to murder their spouse...'

Her eyes drifted to the poster. 'I don't know,' she said softly. 'If you were to examine the situation a bit more closely, perhaps you'd have a bit of empathy for her. Things aren't always what they seem.'

He was thoughtful for a moment, and then shrugged. He felt his nerves deserting him, but forced himself to smile and meet her gaze.

'I see the questions in your eyes, and I'm prepared to answer them.'

'Well, um,' Adam began, unable to meet her stare. 'I suppose I do have a question. Why me?'

Evelyn nodded, as if it were a fair question. 'Does it matter?'

He took another sip of wine, letting the flavour splash around in his mouth. 'I don't get it,' he said. 'Why did you choose to go home with me tonight? There were tons of good-looking guys in that place, but you were smiling at me. Why?'

She was quiet a long time. 'You seemed…nice.'

Adam snorted.

'No, really,' she said. 'Some people have an inner glow; do you know what I'm talking about? They emanate their personality from the outside in. I could tell you were a good guy…and a great lover.'

Adam swayed a little, his nerve faltering. 'But – you don't understand.'

She raised an eyebrow. 'Oh?'

He set the wine down, forcing himself to look her in the eye. 'I don't know what kind of lover I am. I'm a virgin.'

There was a pause.

'I intend to change that.'

Adam shook his head. 'Now I don't know if I can do it. I'm intimidated as hell, quite frankly. I've wanted to make love to a woman for so long, and now you're here, beautiful and mysterious and sensual…'

'Don't forget horny,' she added. 'Adam, I understand if you're a tad apprehensive. But look at the situation this way: you're with a woman that is quite turned on to find out you're a clean slate and now wants to ravish you like an animal. I can see fierceness behind those hazel eyes, and I have no doubt you're fully capable of making me pant. Do you know I'm wet already?'

'Y – you are?'

'Would you like to feel?'

She took his hand in hers, parting her legs and peeling back the chiffon fabric that draped across her thighs. He braced himself to feel the softness of cotton panties – perhaps a satin thong. Instead his fingertips glided across *her*.

'Oh, God,' he murmured. His breath was sucked sharply to the back of his throat.

'I can't – I shouldn't,' he croaked. 'I don't know you very well yet. It wouldn't be right. I would never want you to think that I was only interested in…in…'

She guided his hand lightly across her sex, teasing the velvet folds with his fingers. Adam could feel the throbbing, the dizziness swirling through his head.

'Alright,' she whispered eyes, half-closed. 'If it makes you feel any better, I'm a Gemini, my favourite food is sushi, and I love children. Now that we've gotten to know each other, why don't you feel me from the inside?'

She plunged his finger deep inside of her. They both cried out, she in pleasure, he in shock. Adam felt her wetness smothering his finger and the room started to spin. His eyes rolled upward, the lashes fluttering slightly. He felt his body swaying.

'Adam,' she murmured. 'Are you alright?'

He tried to speak, to reassure her, but his lips wouldn't move.

'Adam?'

His body slumped forward, his head crashing down upon her lap. A long, low moan fell from his lips. He could smell her sweetness; it flooded his nostrils and soothed his senses as his stomach heaved and twisted. He felt her run a tender hand through his hair as his eyes slumped shut.

His vision was sharpening. Rope. Winding around his body. Digging into his flesh. What was he lying against? It was hard, a cold slab. But it didn't make sense...

Scattered around the living room were clusters of candles, their glow stinging his eyes and doubling his dizziness. He felt his stomach churning, thought he might throw up. Breathing deeply, he gritted his teeth and rode out the wave of nausea.

Her voice pricked his ears, floating out from the shadows. 'Be still and don't struggle. I drugged you, Adam. You'll feel wretched for a while, but the sickness will pass.'

He tilted his head and strained his eyes until he saw her, sitting in the velvet armchair, watching him. The violet of her eyes pierced through the darkness, making him shudder. Adam compelled himself to speak, but managed only a low, gurgling noise.

'Your voice will return shortly,' she said. 'Don't strain it.'

She rose and stepped forward. She moved fluidly through the darkness, like a panther, her features illuminated as the moonlight fell across her face. She stared down at him. Her expression was unreadable.

Finally she knelt beside his rigid body, and he could see that her eyes were soft.

'I – I normally just do it,' she said. 'I offer no explanation, and by the time it's over the man thinks he's gone insane – that he had imagined it all.'

She smoothed a lock of his hair with her palm.

'But you're different, Adam. I meant what I said earlier. You have a genuine goodness about you.'

Adam steadied himself against the slab. He felt his throat swelling, and this time when he tried to speak he managed to choke out words.

'Don't…understand…'

She nodded. 'And it's because of your goodness that I'll do something rare for you. I'll let you understand.'

Evelyn settled herself on the carpet. She was quiet a long time, looking hesitant, as if she didn't know where to begin.

'I'm doing this not because I want to,' she murmured. 'But because I have to.'

'Do –' he coughed. 'Do what?'

She placed a hand on his arm. 'Please don't be afraid. I'm not going to kill you.'

This sentence, of course, made him very afraid.

'You're a religious man?' she asked. 'A Christian, yes?'

'Y – yes. Kind of,' he whispered.

'It's alright,' she smiled. 'Most people fall into the kind of category.'

He blinked hard, trying to see her face through the dimness.

She noted his problem. 'Too dark?' she asked. 'I prefer the dark, to be honest. But perhaps you'll feel a bit more comfortable with a bit of light.'

She waved her hand and Adam watched as the candles surrounding them began to grow, tripling in height before his eyes. He let out a terrified squeak as the large flames lapped at the ceiling, overwhelming the room in a searing glow.

'What's happening?' he rasped. 'How did you – what are you?'

She tilted her eyes toward the floor. 'I don't entirely know,' she said softly. 'But I can try my best to help you understand what I must do now.'

Adam's senses had been shocked into alertness.

'Untie me.'

She shook her head. 'I won't. Ask again and I'll simply carry out my plans without explanation. You want to hear my explanation, correct?'

The ropes were too thick, too tight. Struggling would be futile, he knew.

He returned his gaze to her and tried to make sense of what he had just seen. 'Are you some kind of witch?'

Evelyn gave a sad little smile.

'No.'

'What then?'

She looked off in the distance, staring out the window at the palm trees, their leaves tossed helplessly by the wind.

'You are familiar with the Bible?'

Adam narrowed his eyes. 'I guess. The major stuff, anyway.'

'You remember the first chapter? The story of creation?'

He shrugged.

'Listen carefully,' she said, her tone serious. 'The bible is a document not different to a collection of fairy tales. There's a bit of truth to it, but please believe me when I tell you that the stories are wrong. Here is how humanity came to be…'

She took a long breath, the weight of her story heavy in her eyes. 'God created earth, God created Adam. He designed a secluded garden for Adam to live in, but as the days passed Adam found his existence tedious without companionship. He became so distraught by the loneliness that one day he climbed a willow tree and wrapped a long vine around his neck. As he was about to hang himself, God spoke to him. "Why do you wish to die?" God asked. Adam replied, "Because life holds no joy for me. Because this paradise is empty without companionship." God said, "Shall I give you another man for friendship?" But Adam shook his head and said, "What good would another man be? Then the both of us would sit, bored, passing our days in the same manner." Finally God said, "I will give you a companion alike in soul but different in body. She will fill your days with pleasure, and attend to your every desire." And Adam agreed.'

Adam's forehead crinkled. He was about to ask what this tale had to do with their present situation, but she continued.

'And so from Adam's rib, Eve was born. Adam was delighted by her, awed by her beauty, bewitched by her body. God told them both that paradise was theirs, but they must never eat from the golden apple tree by the lake. If they did, they would be banished from the garden for ever. They agreed, and were left to their own devices. Eve was shy and overwhelmed by her strange existence, and she turned to Adam for reassurance. He wrapped his hand round her hair and pulled her to the ground. She screamed and fought wildly, but he took her cruelly, mounting her in the mud. When he had finished, he told her, "You sprang from my body, and are my property to do with as I please. You will serve me however I see fit, and if ever you object, I will punish you until you recognize your place."

Eve was crying, and he sneered and left her there, and went lumbering off to bathe himself in the river.'

Adam thought her mad – she had to be. Where on earth had she heard this story? He may not have been a church regular, but he knew the story of creation.

'The days passed and Adam found great pleasure in his new companion,' she went on. 'He violated her body frequently, and sometimes he would beat her until she couldn't stand, simply for the novelty of it. In the night Eve cried quietly, cursing her wretched existence. Then one day while Adam napped in the afternoon sunlight, she went on a walk down by the lake, down by the golden apple tree. Through the tall grass came a serpent, slithering up her leg, circling her waist, until it draped across her shoulders and its tongue tickled her ear. "Why do you cry?" it asked, to which she replied, "Because I loathe my existence. Because I hate this place, because I want to be free of Adam's cruelty." "Escape," said the serpent. "When the night falls, flee the garden." "I cannot," she replied sadly. "There are walls surrounding the garden, so high one could never hope to climb them. Once when Adam was asleep, I spent all day trying to dig beneath them, but they stretch down to the very centre of the earth." The snake turned her head toward the apple tree. "Eat the forbidden fruit and you will be free," he said. She took an apple from the tree and sank her teeth into its flesh. Suddenly the earth began to shake, and the clouds parted. God's voice came down and said to her, "You have eaten the fruit forbidden to you, and now you shall be exiled for ever. Flee now, or the punishment shall be death." Eve heard the walls crumbling in the distance, and hope filled her bosom. She looked into the serpent's eyes and smiled. "Thank you," she said. "From this day forward my life is my own." The serpent kissed her cheek with his tongue, and she set him upon the ground, and then sprinted toward the distance. Suddenly the vastness of the world became known to her.'

She reached forward and tilted his cheek so that his gaze met hers.

'But,' her voice was raw with urgency. 'That night, as she slept cold and naked in a cave miles away, a bright light woke her. When her eyes opened an angel stood before her, gleaming with heavenly splendour. The angel said to her, "Woman made from Adam, you have been banished from God's paradise, and now your will is your own. But because you drove Adam mad with lust, then left him in agony, your punishment shall not end with banishment. You shall be immortally cursed, unable to die, but bitter to be alive. Every five hundred years, you must commit the very sin that was your undoing: you must tempt a virgin, and then lie with him, or else you *shall* perish by the end of that year, condemned to an eternity in hell." '

Adam's mind was spinning. *She's insane*, he thought. *The girl's completely nuts!*

Evelyn leaned close, so that her sweet breath wafted across his cheek.

'My name isn't Evelyn.' She paused. 'It's Eve.'

Adam would have laughed if his chest didn't hurt so badly.

'Uh huh,' he glared. 'You're the first woman to ever exist. And you now happen to be a twenty-something club hopper in Miami.'

Her eyes grew dark. 'You don't have to listen,' she spat. 'I'll get what I need from you – whether you believe me or not.'

'What do you need from me?' he asked, dreading the answer.

97

'Your lust,' she said. 'I need you inside me, need your virginity. Weren't you listening?'

Adam frowned. 'So this is – it's been five hundred years since you had sex?'

'Well,' she smiled. 'Five hundred years since I've had sex out of necessity.'

'Look Evelyn,' he glared. 'I *wanted* to have sex with you tonight. You didn't have to drug me and hogtie me.'

Evelyn shook her head.

'On the contrary, there are some elements of this liaison that you might object to, and I can't have you fleeing into the night. I'll give you fair warning: there will be pleasure, but there will also be pain. I'm no longer concerned with whether you believe my biography – in five minutes you'll know the truth. Let's begin…'

'Wait!' he cried. 'What did you mean when you said there'd be pain? What the hell are you going to do?'

She gave him an empathetic look. 'I apologize for the pain, but there is no other way. Do you remember what I told you earlier? I won't kill you. After this is done, I promise I'll release you unharmed. You see Adam, even if you wanted to shout your ordeal to the world, no one would believe you.'

She went to the kitchen, and Adam heard her shuffling through items on the counter. When she returned she was holding a ruby apple, the flesh glistening in the candlelight.

'And so it begins,' she said, a note of sadness in her voice. 'Try not to strain yourself. Be brave, Adam.'

'What the hell is the matter with you?' he yelled. 'Let me go you crazy –'

He fell silent when the apple began to emit an eerie glow, subtle at first, but within seconds the light was blinding. Evelyn slit its flesh with her fingernail, and then held the fruit above Adam's mouth. They watched as an electric red droplet of juice trickled from the fruit and dangled over Adam's mouth.

'Open your mouth,' she coaxed.

'So I can drink from a fruit that glows in the dark? Go to hell!'

She snarled, grabbing his hair and yanking until his mouth flew open in a scream of pain.

'I'm not going to hell,' she hissed. 'And tonight you're the reason why.'

The little drop of juice tumbled onto his lips, hitting his flesh with a sharp splat. The juice snaked its way across his tongue, leaving a searing trail as it lunged down his throat.

'Be brave, Adam,' Evelyn whispered. 'Be brave.'

He felt his body contort as the juice surged through his veins, twisting them like poison. A red glow emanated from his flesh; he shrieked at the sight of it. His stomach heaved and quivered, his legs thrashed wildly. His wrists twisted against the ropes like an animal caught in a trap.

Adam's body was too wracked with pain to notice that Evelyn had placed her hand on his forehead. By the time the convulsions had ceased his body was thick with sweat, his lungs struggling to gulp in air.

'W – what was that?' he said, his voice breaking.

'Sin,' Evelyn answered.

She fetched a knife from the kitchen and began to cut the clothes from his body, careful not to slice the ropes. Adam continued to cough and shake.

'I like you, Adam,' she said, slicing the denim from his legs. 'I'm not just going to use your body tonight – not like the others. You're a good man, and for that reason I'm going to make love to you.'

As the stabbing pains in his abdomen began to ebb, he cast his eyes upon his captor, and was surprised to find Evelyn unzipping her dress. The slinky fabric tumbled down her collarbone, sinking to the floor in a rush. The soft curves of her breasts caught the moonlight as she took a step forward, standing before him, presenting herself. His eyes darted to the dark triangle below her navel, as black as her hair, gleaming with the smallest amount of moisture. Pained though he was, he couldn't help but acknowledge her beauty, his eyes combing over her curves with a sense of awe.

But he had little time to marvel at her body; she was already climbing on top of him, her pale thighs straddling his torso. He flinched as she leaned toward him, and her sex rubbed against his, leaving a warm, wet trail as it glided forward. Her breasts hovered so close to his mouth that he could see his breath warming her nipples, prickling them into tautness.

His head was swimming by the time she placed her hand on his chin, tilting his head back so that she could look into his eyes, an epic sadness in her face.

'I wish...I wish it didn't have to be like this. Please don't hate me, Adam.'

He saw a tear glistening in the corner of her eye.

'I don't hate you, Evelyn,' he whispered. 'A moment ago I thought you were crazy, but not now.'

She managed a weak smile. 'Are you ready?'

He was surprised to find that he was not only ready, but willing.

'Y – yes,' he said softly. 'Will there be much more pain – like before?'

Evelyn nodded. She brushed her lips against his, and he found himself stifling a low moan. His lips parted, welcoming the wetness of her tongue, the heat of her kiss.

He strained his neck against the ropes, tasting as much of her as he could.

When at last she pulled away Adam gasped; her skin was illuminating: an electric, rosy glow. His eyes darted to his own flesh and he found himself in the same state.

'What's happening?'

'Don't be afraid, Adam.'

She bent down and her nipple slid between his lips. Before he could think, his tongue was swirling around the tip, his lips sucking in her sweetness. Every time his tongue lapped at her flesh, he felt tiny prickles, as if there were an electric charge coursing through her. It became so strong that he began to wince, but he refused to part with her, licking and sucking until he felt himself grow weak.

When she guided his head back against the slab, her breast wet with his saliva, she had a serene expression. Her look was infectious, and despite himself, Adam felt his lips mirror her smile.

With their bodies lighting up the room like pale stars, Evelyn eased herself backwards until her sex hovered above his own. He was frightened, yes, but now he was consumed by another kind of pain. Her eyes shifted to his hardness, and as she began to ease her hips down toward the source of his aching, a tiny drop of her moisture tumbled down, trickling across his manhood – he groaned at the warmth of it – until he bit his lower lip to stifle a whimper.

'Ignore what you see,' she whispered. 'Ignore what you hear. Look at me, Adam. Keep your eyes on me.'

She tilted her pelvis until she was pressing against him, and she began rubbing herself back and forth, painting him in her wetness. He felt his body melting into the cold stone.

'Oh, God – Evelyn…'

Her eyes were sparkling with something that almost appeared to be adoration. Cupping his cheek in her palm, she dipped her head low, and her lips brushed across his forehead.

Then she pressed her body to his, coaxing him deep inside. He could feel her heat even before she engulfed him, taking him in slowly, letting him savour her inch by inch. When he felt himself completely encased by her she was still for a long moment, eyes half-closed, relishing the weight of him inside her. She looked down at him—a fallen angel—her hair pouring like a river over her shoulders, brushing against his chest.

The story she had told him earlier began to flash through his mind, and suddenly he was picturing her pressed against the dirt, her nails digging into the earth in terror, as she was taken without love, without the slightest tenderness. And now Adam wanted to take her in his arms and cradle her to him, to take her slowly and gently, to stroke her hair and let soft words waft upon her ears. But he felt the ropes rubbing against his flesh and the thought faded from his mind.

He looked into her violet eyes, not daring to blink, as she began to rock her hips. His wrists strained against the bonds. He arched his back, stealing as much contact as he could.

Adam could hear the pants that came in a rush from her lips, could see the beads of sweat gathering on her forehead. But he became aware of another sound – a low, almost inaudible hiss – that was echoing like a choir around him. It was getting louder...closer. He broke away from Evelyn's gaze, and what he saw made the blood freeze in his veins.

From all corners of the room they were pouring down – serpents with scales as sharp as knives. They were plummeting from the ceiling, coiling in piles, slithering over the furniture and across the carpet.

He opened his mouth to scream, but Evelyn covered his lips with her hand, whispering quickly 'Don't look, Adam. They won't harm you. Don't look at them – look at me.'

She was grinding against him faster, moving her hips in frantic little circles. He swallowed a moan and tried to ignore the writhing creatures surrounding them. But by this point there were hundreds of them, and now they clustered around the slab; he felt one of them brush against his torso, dragging its scales slowly across his flesh, and his eyes clamped shut as he waited for the creature to slide away.

There was a piercing crack – like lightning – from above. Adam's eyes flashed open and flew to the ceiling. He screamed. A swirling red cloud hovered over them, crackling and churning in a fury of light.

The hysteria in his voice cut through the roar of the cloud. 'Evelyn!'

She ignored him, thrusting faster. The wind beating down from above whipped her hair into a dark frenzy.

'Evelyn!' he screamed.

'It's alright,' she called. 'No harm will come to you!'

Adam gritted his teeth. He felt the pressure below, felt the ache in his groin reaching a fever pitch. Evelyn grunted with determination; she seemed to sense how close he was to exploding. Around them the hiss of the serpents became deafening, rattling the walls and shaking the slab. Her breasts were bobbing up and down so frantically that the nipples became a rosy blur, her thrusts unrelenting. He felt himself start to twitch, and Evelyn felt it too. She plunged down with a force so violent that he could feel the orgasm being sucked from his body. His skull dug into the slab. A howl echoed from his throat and the walls rumbled with his scream.

Evelyn's head shot backward. Her eyes slammed shut. She clenched down, squeezing out every droplet from deep inside of him. He felt a wave of electricity tearing through her body – a jolt of pain so profound that she began to sob, her shoulders heaving uncontrollably. She tried frantically to steady herself with her legs, and for a moment she seemed so weak that she would fall to the floor in a trembling heap. The bellowing cloud above them exploded in a deafening burst, smothering the room in a crimson fog as the snakes rolled onto their bellies, twitching and screaming in a shrill chorus.

Adam felt a stabbing pain inside his chest, as if his bones were unhinging within his body, then a jagged pressure inside his throat—something burrowing its way toward his mouth. His jaw opened wide. He coughed and retched until he felt the hard object tumble from his mouth, landing with a sharp thud on his chest where the pain had originated. He stared incredulously at the rib, sticky with his saliva.

The red mist was dissipating. Adam's eyes darted to the floor, relieved to find that the serpents had vanished. He took a deep breath.

'Adam?'

Her voice was uneven, scratched. He looked up to see her eyes stained with tears.

'Are you okay?'

He nodded.

She dabbed at her eyes with her fingers. Then with shaking hands she took the rib and held it close to her face. She seemed lost in thought, eyes cloudy for a long time before she finally spoke again.

'It's over now,' she said. 'I'll untie you.'

He felt himself sliding out of her warmth, her wetness. She knelt beside him and wiped the sweat from his brow.

'I'm sorry, Adam,' she said. 'You don't deserve such pain. I wish I had chosen someone else–some muscle-covered jock with a contemptible personality. I've never done this with anyone like you.' She gave him a smile tinged with irony. 'They say you always remember your first…'

'I – I feel so weak.'

'It'll pass,' she assured him.

She kissed his cheek.

He managed to give her a feeble smile. 'I understand, Evelyn,' he whispered. 'You had to do this. I'll never hate you for it.'

The words made her lips tremble. 'I – thank you.'

She grabbed the knife from the floor and began cutting through the ropes that wrapped around his legs.

'Let me see you again,' he blurted.

She almost dropped the knife. 'W – what?'

His eyes were earnest. 'I said I want to see you again.'

Evelyn shook her head quickly.

'No,' she whispered. 'Don't you understand? I'm cursed. Damned. I can't stay in the same place for more than five years; lest people become aware of the way my body refuses to age. You need to go home now, Adam. Forget what happened here tonight. It was a dream.'

'But –'

'No!' she said her tone serious. 'I don't have friends and I certainly don't have boyfriends.'

'Don't you ever get lonely? Want someone to confide in? Evelyn, please – I won't leave until you agree to see me again.'

She moved toward his face, her eyes like open wounds as she studied him. She could see the resolve in his expression. She tousled his hair with her fingers. A tear clung to the corner of her eye; when she blinked it trailed down her cheek and across her lips.

'Goodbye, Adam.'

He felt her hand tighten around his hair, wrenching his head forward. When she brought it down hard against the slab, her mournful eyes were the last thing he saw before everything went dark.

When his eyelids fluttered open, he wasn't sure where he was at first–the room was bare, stripped of furniture and paintings. His head was ringing. He felt the carpet beneath his fingers and he turned his head to find that there were no ropes, no slab – no Evelyn. But his eyes caught a crumpled piece of paper lying several feet away, and he lurched toward it, his head reeling. He brought the note close to his face and his eyes frantically combed the words.

Dear Adam,

Please forgive me. I had to. Friends are a danger I cannot afford. Please understand. Though I doubt it will lift your spirits, I want you to know that I genuinely enjoyed being with you, and I know you'll find happiness in this world of cruelty and degradation. Don't worry about tidying up after yourself – I'm abandoning the apartment for good. I've had enough of the sun and the ocean. I'm thinking somewhere where there's snow. Perhaps Europe...

Love,

Evelyn

He let his body sink to the floor. As he took deep, ragged breaths, the faint scent of apples curled around his nostrils as he sobbed into the carpet.

'*Bound*' To Sell
by Teresa Joseph

Having worked at the company for almost three years and having made no attempt to hide the fact that I was a lesbian, I suppose that it didn't come as much of a surprise when one of the other women came over to ask me if I had a lot of lesbian friends.

More than just idle curiosity, however, it turned out that Sally was also a lesbian and that, to my initial horror, she made a bit of extra cash holding sales parties in the evenings and at weekends. But rather than selling Amway, Tupperware or any of that rubbish, I actually breathed a sigh of relief when she told me that she sold fetish bondage gear.

Of course, before you can hold any type of party, the first things that you need are some guests and a place for them to go. And so in exchange for a share of the takings, I agreed to invite my friends to my house the following weekend and play the dutiful hostess.

On the night of the party, having dolled myself up, bought half a dozen bottles of wine and laid out a wide variety of snacks, I waited for all my friends to arrive. And then, resisting the urge to ruin my lipstick with a little lesbian foreplay, I did my best to keep things civilized until the saleswoman turned up.

'Good evening, ladies.' She greeted us warmly as she made her way up to the front of the room and opened up her sample case. 'My name is Sally, and I'm here to help make your sex lives even more exciting than they are now.'

Having already drunk a few glasses of wine by that point, it was difficult for me to tell the difference between my friends and a gang of immature schoolgirls as they sat whispering and giggling around the room. And so when the saleswoman asked for someone to step forward and help her demonstrate what she had to offer, as well as being the hostess I was also the only one who was sober enough to volunteer.

A few moments later, once Sally had fastened ten normal looking black leather straps around my wrists, elbows, thighs, knees and ankles and a belt around my waist, I was groaning with satisfaction as she tied a smooth leather collar around my neck and fitted me with a soft rubber ball-gag. And as I stood there savouring the tingle in my pussy, the saleswoman turned me to face the audience so that the presentation could begin.'

'The 'Ultrabond 2000' system is a revolution in fetish bondage play,' announced Sally, taking a remote controller from her case and asking me to hold my wrists up so that everyone could see. 'Because while it might look like a collection of ordinary leather straps, it gives you absolute control over your lover's body and *literally* puts her under your thumb.'

The next thing I knew, the straps on my wrists had pulled together like a pair of magnets. And although I tried to pull them apart, it was as if they were locked together and there was nothing that I could do.

'Simply by pressing this button,' Sally continued, 'I've activated two of the electromagnets that are inside the leather of this woman's wrist straps, forcing them to lock together no matter how much she might try to resist.'

And as they watched me struggle in the vain attempt to separate my wrists, my friends stopped giggling and looked on in absolute silence; worried that this was all just part of a confidence trick, but eager to see what else these leather straps could do.

'But of course, each strap has more than one set of magnets.'

And before I knew it, my ankles had been locked together and my wrists had been pulled down to link with them as well.

'And you can unlock one set of magnets without unlocking the others as well.'

Standing in my own living room, gagged and trussed up like a Christmas Turkey as my friends looked on, I was relieved that Sally switched off some of the magnets before I lost my balance. However although my ankles and wrists were no longer fastened to *each other*, now that she'd fastened my knees to my elbows so that I couldn't bend my legs, it still looked as if I was reaching down to grab hold of my ankles and I was still as helpless as could be.

'Now, I realize that you might be sceptical,' said Sally as she endeavoured to reassure my friends that this really wasn't a trick. 'And so please feel free to come up here and inspect the straps for yourselves.'

But as I stood there bound and gagged, in a position that practically begged my friends to spank my bottom and reach up the back of my skirt, since I already knew that I was helpless, I really felt as though I was the one who needed to be reassured.

One of my friends came up to 'inspect' the equipment, gently caressing my helpless body and causing me to groan with delight.

'Does that feel good? If I reached down to stroke your pussy, would you try to stand back up?'

But not even waiting to see if I nodded or shook my head, a few moments later I was whimpering loud enough for the whole room to hear as she gently reached up the back of my skirt, pushed the crotch of my knickers to one side and began stroking my juicy, wet slit.

'And what if I gave you a spanking?' she teased, still fingering my pussy as she used her free hand to hitch my skirt up around my waist and smack my pert, round rump.

By that point, I think I was so horny that even if I had been able to stand up, I would still have just held onto my ankles and let the woman have her way. But as it was, however, there was no way that I could stand up until Sally deactivated the cuffs.

Of course, there was still a long way to go until the end of the presentation. And so a few minutes later, once everyone had come up to see just how helpless I really was and savoured my moans of satisfaction for themselves, the saleswoman finally deactivated the cuffs. And once she'd given me a chance to smooth my skirt down and push my hair back away from my face, she carried on with the presentation and proved just how much of a puppet I'd actually become.

'If your lover is pretending to be your French maid, then by pressing this combination of buttons, you can make her stand like this.'

And as a magnet in the strap of my ball gag was activated, pulling it down towards my collar and making it look as if I was bowing my head, I felt my knees and ankles pull together, my elbows become locked to the sides of my waist and my wrists bind together as they had done before. And before I knew it, as much as I might have tried to struggle, I was suddenly a meek little serving girl, standing respectfully with my head bowed and my hands in my lap, waiting for my mistress's command.

And if you want her to beg like a loving little puppy...'

I actually whimpered as, after an extremely brief moment of freedom, I was literally pulled down onto my knees as the straps on my thighs were pulled towards the straps around my ankles. And as my head was pulled back by the magnet in my collar, my elbows were pinned back to my waist and wrists were pulled up under my chin in the perfect begging position.

The saleswoman playfully scratched me behind my ears, evoking delighted howls of ecstasy from every one of my friends.

'Who's a cute little puppy?'

I knelt there feeling the juice from my pussy begin to ruin the cloth of my skirt and knickers. The magnet in my collar meant that I had no choice but to look up at her, gazing lovingly into her eyes.

Of course, I wasn't the only one who was feeling horny. And so as my friends all uncrossed their legs to finger their dripping wet pussies, too mesmerized by what they saw to want to fuck each other but too horny not to wank, Sally quickly slipped off her knickers as she decided to put my new obedience to good use.

Allowing me to move just enough to crawl up to her seat, the saleswoman then used the remote control to force me to kneel down in front of her with my wrist cuffs pinned to the back of my belt. And once she had removed my ball gag and given me a long loving kiss, she ordered me to lick her naked pussy, and I eagerly obeyed.

At this point, I feel I must confess that, no matter how long I might live, I don't think that I'll ever experience something so intensely erotic as being completely bound and helpless while licking the pussy of a woman who's taken complete control of your body. And as I began to submit completely to Sally's slightest whim, I realized that as well as control of her body, she was also taking control of my mind, of my heart and of my soul.

Even when I had finished licking the saleswoman's pussy and she had the deactivated all of the magnets to allow me to take a break, I still knelt there like an obedient little sex toy, ready and willing to obey her every command. But although it looked as if the presentation was over, there was still one last thing that she needed to demonstrate.

'Oh dear, I almost forgot,' giggled Sally as her finger hovered over one of the buttons on the remote control. 'If you want to reward your gorgeous little sex toy, then all that you have to do is *this*.'

The moment that she touched the button, I climaxed so hard that I almost saw the gates of heaven as an extremely mild shock of electricity began to surge through me, causing every inch of my body to tingle and stimulating me to a point of ecstasy that I had never imagined possible.

'Also, if you want to kiss your lover or let her lick your pussy at the same time, then you can enjoy her reward as well.'

And when one of my friends came over to give me a kiss and Sally pressed the button for a second time, we both began to squeal with orgasm as the surge shot through both of us like a bolt of pure joy.

Despite the fact that the presentation was now over and we were all desperate to buy, we were all so desperately horny that I would have been willing to carry on licking everyone's pussies for the rest of my natural life. And so once my friends had all taken off their knickers and I had rolled over onto my back with my ankles fastened to my wrists, Sally literally ripped off my skirt and knickers and we all descended into an orgy that I'll never be able to forget.

As each of my friends then took it in turns to sit on my face or kneel down between my legs to lick my own dripping pussy, Sally stood watch over us with the remote control, forcing us to climax over and over again as she sent a surge of electricity through each of our willing slits. And for the next seven unforgettable hours, as we all, licked and fisted each other's pussies to the point of unconsciousness, and Sally's device forced us all to climax over and over again, I am proud to say that I remained the obedient little sex toy until the very end.

The next day however, having dragged my exhausted body into work as usual but still grinning from ear to ear like the mindless little sex toy that I had become, when Sally asked if I would like to host another sales party the next week, I simply had no choice but to refuse.

'Please mistress,' I whimpered pitifully. 'Please let me have two weeks to rest before we have another party. I don't think that my pussy could take any more.'

After The Funeral
by Elizabeth Cage

Although she would never admit it to anyone else, Claudia was actually relieved when Mark died. Theirs had not been what you would call a fulfilled marriage. She had never been too keen on sex, so she could hardly complain when he sought his pleasure elsewhere. But it was his attempts to introduce her, convert her, to practices she thought were just plain wrong that really annoyed her. I mean, tying someone up before making love to them – what was that all about?

'At least he didn't suffer,' her sister, Helen, said in an effort to comfort her, though she didn't need comforting.

His BMW had crashed into a wall, head on. Brake failure.

The police and insurance people had finally satisfied themselves that it had been an accident, despite the fact that Claudia would inherit the Harrington fortune after her husband's unfortunate demise.

'So, how much did he leave you?' asked Helen.

Claudia eyed her sister curiously. Was she hoping for a handout because she was family?

'The town house, the country house, the villa, multiple investments. An obscene amount, I hope,' she replied.

'Although I won't know for sure until I speak to the solicitor. He asked me to come in later today, to sort out the paperwork.'

The office of Elliott Westerham and Associates was in the city centre, a big Edwardian converted house, tastefully decorated. Mark and Elliott had got on well socially and Elliott had visited the house on occasions, so they were on first name terms. But, for some reason, today Claudia was aware that he was regarding her oddly, as if he was uneasy in her company.

'Elliott.'

'Claudia.'

He looked and sounded formal in his pin-striped business suit. He handed her an envelope.

'Mark left this with me. You were to have it after his death.'

'Is it to do with the will?' she asked, with a little too much enthusiasm.

'Open it.'

He was making her uncomfortable, staring at her. She ripped open the envelope, keen to get the legal affairs over with. As she started to read, her mouth dropped open. Eventually, when she had read the letter twice more, she looked at Elliott.

'Is this a joke?'

'No joke. Mark was deadly serious, excuse the pun.'

'So you're saying that unless I respect Mark's last wishes, I won't get a penny.'

'Correct.'

'But have you seen what he's asking me to do?'

He blushed. 'Yes.'

'Did you put him up to this?'

'Of course not. Mark was very strong-willed, you know that.'

'I can't. It's just too…God, I don't even want to think about it.'

'Then Mark's entire estate goes to the Donkey Sanctuary.'

'Now that is obscene.'

'You have until tomorrow midday to make your decision. Go home, sleep on it.'

Of course, she couldn't sleep a wink, cursing Mark for treating her like this. He knew her views on anything she regarded as remotely kinky. She had made that very clear. The next day, she went back to Elliott's office, having carefully considered what the money would get her and trying to imagine life without it.

'I'll do it. Under protest, of course.'

'Of course. I'll make the necessary arrangements.'

'Thank you. But I don't see why you have to be there.'

'I have to witness the proceedings, to ensure Mark's will is respected. I hope you understand.'

The house was in a cul-de-sac – an upmarket but otherwise ordinary looking house in a relatively affluent part of town. She allowed herself a nervous smile. She had visualised a gothic mansion. Her fingers kept involuntarily reaching up to touch the leather collar around her neck. She wasn't used to being restricted in any way at all. Part of her wanted to tear it off, yet a part of her that had always remained hidden felt a strange comfort.

She shuddered as Elliott helped her out of the car, her thin black slip clinging to the contours of her firm and supple body. No underwear, just a pair of shiny high heels. All part of Mark's instructions. He had been very precise in his requirements. A stickler for detail. What she wouldn't do for him in life he was going to make her go through anyway. She wondered if he was laughing from his new home beyond the grave, wherever that might be.

The door was opened by a very tall woman in a tight rubber dress and heavy make-up, who gestured her and Elliott up the stairs to a warm room, lit by candles. Swathes of red silk were draped across the walls and floor. The air was heavy with exotic incense.

A large mirror lined one wall. In the centre of the room was a small wooden table, draped with a velvet cloth.

'Sit down.' She was taken aback at Elliott's firm tone.

As she moved forward he said, 'No, take off your slip first.'

'I can't.'

'You must. Mark's instructions were quite explicit.'

How could she let Elliott see her naked? Perhaps this was all a bad dream and any moment now she would wake up.

Elliott regarded her gravely. 'Take it off,' he repeated.

With a sulky pout, she let the slip fall to the ground and stepped out of it.

'Now you can get on the table.'

Claudia felt his eyes burning into her. Her face flushed crimson, she had to look away to avoid his gaze. She was seething. If it wasn't for the money...

'Kneel. Leave your shoes on. Spread your knees.'

It felt awkward to sit in such an exposed position on the small table, and acutely embarrassing, but she did it.

'Now, you do have a choice about the next bit. You can watch everything that happens to you or be blindfolded.'

She hesitated. She wanted to see what was going to happen because she hated surprises. But on the other hand, she couldn't bear to look at herself naked and vulnerable.

'I'll take the blindfold.'

A soft red cloth was placed over her eyes.

She heard the door open, someone else enter the room. A man's voice. Unfamiliar. She guessed it must be the nawashi, the rope master.

'Is she ready?'

'Yes. You can start now.'

She trembled as she felt her arms pinned behind her back, rope biting into the soft flesh of her wrists. Then more rope – or was it from the same length – wrapped around her waist, across her chest, circling her breasts and nipples, pulling tight, momentarily taking her breath away. Then more around her legs, ankles, in an intricate pattern; even the heels of her shoes were bound together.

She winced as rope pinched the insides of her thighs. It hurt. She nearly panicked, feeling a brief flash of claustrophobia before the calm returned.

Then stillness. An amazing stillness. Her body was restricted yet her mind felt strangely liberated, free, as her focus turned inwards, heightening awareness of every sensation.

It was as if she was experiencing her body for the first time: a kind of revelation. Then rope was passed between her legs, grazing her delicate inner lips, like some invisible fingertip. She gasped. Suddenly her entire being became focussed on this area, the slightest pressure magnified tenfold, as if it were the only thing that existed. The only thing.

Unable to move, Claudia's focus travelled to the deep recesses of her inner self; she experienced complete introspection and serenity. In her meditative state, she became vaguely aware of sounds in the room, other voices, male and female: she had no idea how many. She realized that she was being looked at, admired, an object of abstract beauty and wonder.

'She looks stunning.' A woman's voice, almost wistful.

'A work of art.' A man.

'There's a particular intimacy in allowing someone to tie you up. There has to be complete trust that they won't abuse the power you are freely giving them. The intimacy comes from opening yourself psychologically and allowing them to enter, explore and guide.'

Another man. A familiar tone. Surely not Elliott? What would he know about Japanese rope bondage?

'I've heard the experience can be overwhelming, very intense and powerful.'

The first woman again. 'Can I take a photograph?'

Suddenly, Claudia was jerked out of her trance-like state. She wanted to shout 'No way,' but, for some reason, she couldn't speak.

Then she heard Elliott reply, 'Yes, of course.'

She wanted to scream at him, but she was reluctant to abandon this feeling of peace and calm. After all, there was nothing she could to do stop him. She was tied up, helpless. She had to go with the flow. So she let go.

When, finally, an hour or so later, the ropes were removed, one by one, she felt so light-headed she thought she might pass out. She felt a hand reach out to support her, to stop her falling. She didn't want the blindfold to be taken off. She wanted to stay like this. Forever. She did not want to return to the ordinary world. Yet she knew that once her eyes were open again she would feel anything but ordinary. She felt like she had been reborn.

'Are you okay?' asked Elliott.

There was genuine concern in his voice, which both surprised and moved her.

'I don't know.'

She tottered as she placed a foot tentatively on the floor. Her knees buckled.

'Hey, I've got you,' said Elliott.

'Yes. You have.'

She felt as high as a kite. Spaced out. And although the actual ropes were lying in a coil on the floor, like a sleeping snake, she could still feel them around her body.

Glancing at her arms she saw the marks like livid red bangles, deeply embedded.

'The physical marks and feeling stay with you long afterwards,' said Elliott.

How did he know?

'Really?'

She was smiling vaguely, her body rapidly melting. As her legs gave out on her again, Elliott scooped her into his arms and carried her across the landing into a dimly lit bedroom. He laid her gently on the bed and knelt beside her, kissing her lightly on the neck. Looking into his eyes, so dark and intense, she knew that he would make love to her and that it would be very good.

'We can't, not here, not in someone else's bed,' she protested feebly.

'It's my bed,' he replied, tenderly stroking a strand of her copper-red hair.

'Your bed?'

'And my house.'

She blinked back at him, her mind fuzzy.

'Anyway, you're a very rich woman now. You can do whatever you want.'

She sighed. She had actually forgotten about the money. Yet it was the reason she was here, the reason she had allowed this to happen.

'I've wanted you for a long, long time,' he murmured, his lips grazing her cheek. 'I couldn't wait any longer.'

He began to trace the rope marks on her body with his tongue.

She trembled as an unsettling thought struck her. Brake failure, the police said. Unexplained brake failure.

Then the tip of his tongue found the newly sensitive place between her legs and she arched her back and moaned, abandoning herself once more to pure sensation. Any uncertainty she had about Elliott vanished for the time being. There would be plenty of time to think. Later. Much, much later.

Vanilla
by Jade Taylor

I'd never been one to believe that sex was necessarily better with people you were in love with.

Sure, the idea was nice, and there was a little bit of the hopeful romantic even in me that hoped it was true. But I was also practical enough to know that you could have mind-blowing sex with people you weren't madly in love with, or people you didn't even like that much.

Great sex doesn't have to make sense.

But I couldn't understand why, when I finally found someone I liked beyond breakfast, the sex wasn't knocking my socks off.

It wasn't fair.

He was just a little *vanilla* for my tastes.

I was mad on Shaun, I admit it, could have let myself go plunging head over heels for him, but I'd always had that wild streak, that little kink, that stopped me letting go.

That little bit of me saying that I'd get bored, that if we stuck together sooner or later I'd be looking for more adventurous partners (and probably breaking his heart in the process), the part of me that said I'd be doing what I always swore I wouldn't: *settling*.

My ideal man meant ideal sex.

Sure, he knew what he was doing, could work his way through the usual repertoire with no problems, could follow instructions and make me come easy enough, but that was all.

Maybe that was the problem – the *usual* repertoire.

I usually preferred something a little different.

He was a little too technical, always seeming to hold something back, no fire, no passion, no unique selling point that made me think, hey, this one's really *good*.

So there we are, three months down the line, on a dirty weekend in Amsterdam that really wasn't that dirty.

We weren't doing drugs, weren't getting high and having giggly sex, weren't exploring the red light district, weren't taking the seediness of the city and twisting it into our own sexual fantasies.

The most excitement we'd had so far was spotting a man smoking in the Van Gogh museum and his subsequent eviction.

Maybe it was shyness, I thought, trying to give him the benefit of the doubt. He was so funny, so cute, I *liked* him.

But I was getting frustrated.

Maybe there was an animal hidden deep inside just waiting to be released, but right then I was too irritable to care.

Sometimes a girl just needs a good fuck and shyness be damned.

I was fed up of fucking men I didn't like, then finding a man I liked that I didn't like fucking enough.

It was so hot, and although I would have loved to sit down in an air-conditioned bar or coffee shop, football fever seemed to be sweeping the city. I had always hated football, not even the sight of fit men in shorts being able to sway my opinion, and knew I wouldn't be able to tolerate football supporters as they grew louder as they got drunk or high.

My idea of fun was more cuffs and code-words than watching men chasing a ball for ninety minutes.

Then we saw the Torture Museum.

'This looks a little different,' I laughed, knowing that although it wasn't the sort of museum he'd had in mind for this trip, he already knew I'd be a bitch if I didn't get my way.

'Sure,' he nodded hesitantly, fumbling in his wallet for a handful of Euros; still fumbling by the time I took control and paid for us both.

Please God, let the fumbling be just nerves, I thought; please don't let me be fucking a fumbler.

Inside it was deserted, dark and cool, and I reached for his hand as he followed me up the narrow staircase, feeling like a bitch as the air-conditioning hit me.

The rack was first, and as he read the information board aloud I studied the gruesome pictures, wondering why people would invent such a thing.

Then there was the pear, and again he read the information aloud as I ran my hands over the structure, imagining the pain it could cause.

The disturbing thought was lifted by the realization that it looked similar to some of the stuff I'd seen in fetish clubs, the thought that some people had obviously found more pleasurable uses for it.

There were many other devices I'd never heard of, and it made me smile as he paused by the scold's bridle.

'I bet you'd love that, it would stop my moaning,' I laughed, trying to let him know I realized I'd been acting like a cranky bitch, trying to make him relax, hoping that would help things.

'It might help,' he sighed, looking so despondent I couldn't help but go over to him, circling my hands around his waist and standing on tiptoes to kiss his neck.

I knew the effect it would have, knew his hot-spots so well already, and knew that he'd probably tell me to stop, that there were people around, that we should behave ourselves.

Instead he kissed me hard on the mouth, pulling me closer, his tongue touching mine as he relaxed in a way I hadn't expected.

Despite everything I felt a rush of excitement, felt the blood rush to my groin, my pulse quicken.

'I kind of like it when you're moaning,' he whispered, and there was no mistaking his meaning as he nuzzled against my neck, his breath hot on my skin, making me sigh in anticipation.

Maybe there was hope after all, I thought.

I pulled him closer, hooking my leg around him as I finally felt some passion, knowing that there was nobody around to see as I kissed him hard, tongues tangling as I felt him growing hard against me.

I shifted slightly as he began to grind his cock against my stomach, trying to angle myself so he could rub against me. It didn't work until he grabbed my hips, used his strong arm to lift me, rubbing his cock against my swollen lips. My skirt began to ride up, and his hands went beneath it to cup my arse, and I sighed loudly.

Despite my need for something different it was I that pulled away, flustered by the way he was taking control; by the way he was making me react.

By the way my body reacted.

'You're not playing now?' he asked, grabbing me by the wrist, holding me tightly.

'Maybe later,' I replied, sure that later I would get to see more of this passion, that finally I would be truly satisfied.

'What's wrong with now?' he asked, pulling me closer again. I tried to resist, knowing that I could easily get carried away, but when he got close enough to kiss me he instead laughed and stepped away.

I stepped back, puzzled.

'Thought you liked playing games?' he asked, smiling at my confusion.

I blushed – I *never* blush – wondering whether he meant what I thought, what I hoped, and how.

I turned to the next exhibit, hoping to gain my composure while he examined it.

Instead of reading the information aloud as before, he pulled his camera out of his pocket.

'Let's get a picture.'

'Let's not,' I answered; I'd never enjoyed having my photo taken.

I expected him to agree, to submit to me as usual, but instead he grabbed my wrist again and pulled me closer to the exhibit. Instead of pulling away, I had to admit it was a turn-on as I submitted docilely to his demand, and let him bend me over and position me in the stocks so my wrists and neck were caught firmly between the pieces of thick wood.

'One for the mantelpiece,' I tried to laugh, but my mouth was dry and my laugh high-pitched and false as he fastened it securely, so I was completely trapped.

The thought turned me on.

I'd always enjoyed being submissive, and I was already so horny, my clit felt swollen and throbbing before he'd even touched me.

The thought of being so publicly exhibited only served to turn me on further.

I smiled as he took the picture, then the flash momentarily blinded me.

When my eyes adjusted to the darkness I could no longer see him.

'Shaun?' I called quietly, wanting to know where he was, but not wanting to attract the man who'd sold the tickets' attention, not wanting him to find me like this, bent over with my arse in the air, wearing my little denim skirt that covered very little, trapped.

To find me bound and horny.

Despite that, I felt myself getting wetter.

I heard movement behind me, but couldn't turn my head to see who it was.

'Shaun?' I asked again, but when I got no reply I fell silent.

Then I felt hands touch my waist.

Immediately I knew it was Shaun, knew that I was finally going to get something a little less vanilla, and felt my cunt flood with anticipation.

I felt his hands pull at my skirt, leaving it bunched up around my waist, exposing my almost bare arse, my panties so small they were almost non-existent.

For a moment there was nothing, and all I could hear was my breathing, getting heavier and faster as I waited for him to touch me, wanting it so much.

I'd never been hornier.

And then he touched me.

His hand stroked across my arse, slowing as it reached the crack, a finger teasing around my anus, my panties providing no resistance to the intrusion.

Not that I wanted them to.

I moaned softly.

I pushed my arse higher, calves straining as I stood on tiptoe so I could part my legs further, wanting him to move his attention to my swollen clit.

'Please,' I begged, hearing his breath quicken with my pleading request.

I knew he was as horny as me, but he continued teasing me.

Gradually his hand moved forward, finally stroking my clit through the already sodden fabric.

He hooked his fingers around the sides of my thong, pulling down the flimsy material, and I lifted my feet willingly to step out of it.

I was totally exposed, totally trapped, anyone could have walked into the museum and seen my naked cunt and I couldn't have moved, but I didn't want to stop.

I heard a zip, then a rustling of material, then his hands were holding my hips as he stepped closer.

I felt his cock against my bare arse, the tip hot, hard and sticky, and he used his knee to part my legs further, then thrust deep inside me.

He felt expert at it, filling me up then pulling out completely, made me feel like I was nothing but gaping hole and swollen clit. I wanted him to touch me so much, wished my hands were free so I could touch myself as he moved so slowly inside me.

But I was trapped completely.

'Touch me,' I moaned, but instead of touching my clit his hands roughly pushed up my shirt, pushed up my bra and rubbed my nipples roughly as he started to move faster inside me.

'No,' I moaned, wanting to protest more loudly, but knowing that someone could easily hear me and come to investigate. I tried to move away from him, tried to pull away from his cock, but it was useless; I was completely vulnerable like that and unable to move.

The thought made the juices rush down my thighs, and it was his turn to sigh loudly as he felt it.

'Say sorry,' he whispered, moving a hand away from my breasts and finally sliding it between my slick and swollen lips.

'What?' I asked, moving my hips desperately, trying to make him touch me.

'Say you're sorry for being such a moody bitch,' he demanded, fingers teasing my clit, cock thrusting deep inside me.

I would have said anything then, anything to make me come like that.

'I'm sorry,' I apologized, but it wasn't good enough.

'Say it all,' he demanded, his fingers slowing. 'Or you don't get to come.'

His cock moved faster as his fingers moved further away from my clit.

'I'm sorry for being such a moody bitch,' I apologized, and at last he touched my clit. His fingers were firm and steady, caressing my clit with long slow strokes, his cock barely moving inside me then as I knew he was close.

I heard the door open below us, and although I knew I should be insisting Shaun release me, let me tidy myself up, I said nothing, the thought of someone being near turning me on, and as Shaun rubbed harder, thrust harder, I knew he felt the same. Seconds later I came hard, grateful for Shaun still holding me up as my knees went weak, and seconds later Shaun came hard, holding my hips so tightly his fingers left distinct bruises.

But, right then, I felt nothing but excitement.

He pulled away quickly and pulled my skirt down, but still left me in the stocks.

A middle-aged couple came wandering in, and paused to read the information board.

The man looked at Shaun, looked at me, then winked broadly at Shaun.

'This sure has some potential,' he said, his American accent strong.

His wife swatted at him. 'Not everyone thinks like you!'

Shaun took another photo, pretending we were still posing.

And all the time spunk was dribbling down my thighs.

'Will you take a photo of us?' he asked the couple, passing his camera over to the man as he stood by me.

Afterwards they left, and Shaun at last released me.

I rubbed at my neck and wrists, sore from having been in bondage so long.

'Ow,' I moaned. 'That hurt.'

'Are you being cranky again already?' he asked.

I raised an eyebrow, thinking where being cranky had just got me.

'Maybe.'

He smiled

The photo's still on the mantelpiece now.

And now you could never describe Shaun as vanilla…………

Counting To Three In French
by Bryn Allen

He'd met her at a dinner party, one of those half-business, half-pleasure things for the university that had filled too much of his time that summer. The night was hot and Midwest muggy, but for some reason they'd been led outside for after-dinner drinks in the bugs and the flickering light of the citronella torches. He first noticed her then, pretty, tall but rounded with light brown hair and hard green eyes, and he had watched her as she leaned alone against a column on the shadowed patio while his friends chattered around him about movies and health clubs, watched until she had finally dipped into her purse and removed a sleek silver case. She'd popped it open and pulled out one slim dark cigarette, lit it and brought it up slowly to set between her full lips. Her eyes finally met his then, steady over the glowing ember, but he'd made himself look away. Kurt did triathlons. He didn't do smokers.

Now he lay naked in darkness, silken rope wrapped round his wrists and ankles, a blindfold tight on his face. He lay on the floor of the ancient Parisian apartment and could smell the layers, the generations, of smoke that had soaked into the wooden floor and thick plaster, the carpets and battered furniture. Over that ancient scent was a fresh cloud of harsh fume, drifting on the swell of French chatter that came from the next room where Marie was talking with her friends, telling them God knows what, preparing to bring them in here. In here to where he lay, helpless, alone, naked. Hard.

The French had caused it. Kurt didn't know a word, but its shape in Marie's mellow alto had thrown him at that party. After he had looked away, after he thought he'd refused her, she'd walked up and spoken to one of his friends. He'd known she was asking about him by the way her cool eyes slid over his face and body as she spoke, but what they said had been lost to him. Holding his drink in the humid night air, surrounded by others but dreadfully aware of her presence, that sudden sense of helpless ignorance had made him lose track of his aversion to smoky clothes and mouths that tasted of ash. When she'd finally spoken to him in clear English, lightly layered with her native tongue, he heard sensuality and sureness, and deep in it all, command. Later that night he was on his knees in her apartment, mouth on her sex and hands cupping the warm smooth skin of her buttocks, bringing her to climax as she stood and stared down at him past the red coal of her dark cigarette. She had waited until morning before she had finally smoked him, and he'd brought her to orgasm twice more with his hands before that. That was how she wanted it, how she had ordered it, and so that was what he'd done. One night and she owned him, and he bent himself to her will, helpless in his hunger to please her, to bend himself to her desire.

She had returned to Paris in the fall, had left him alone and lost without her sex and loving disdain. Kurt had been dominated before, learning and experimenting with three different women before Marie, but it was different with

133

her. It was easy, nothing played at, just something that was between them. Simple, complete, total. When he first had the chance, he had flown to her, to a smoky city that he had never thought much of before, in a country he had never cared for. Two weeks with Marie, five days already gone, passed in sex, subjugation and cigarette smoke. Trapped in her city, trapped by culture and language, he was helpless in a way he had never been before, dependent on his lover for everything. Marie laughed at his uselessness and made him pay for her help with his tongue, his fingers, and his cock.

In the other room, he heard chairs shuffle, floorboards creak, the sound of the door clicking open. He heard Marie's voice, low and darkly amused, mixed with the sounds of soft laughter and excited French. Kurt couldn't tell how many, one, two, a thousand, they were coming into the room and staring down at him, naked and helpless and blind, so hard and wanting he was already dripping wet warmth down onto his belly. Footsteps surrounded him, soft pad of bare or stockinged feet intermixed with the clatter of heels, then silence as they stopped. Kurt could feel them staring down at him, staring with humour and disdain as they flicked the ash of their stinking Cloves and Marlboros over his bare skin, coating him in the grey dust dandruff of their nicotine angels. Beside his head, the ancient floorboards sighed and popped as someone stepped close to lean down and run a hand through his hair. In her beautiful accented whisper, Marie spoke to him, 'All here now, pet. I want us to play a game with you. Each will have a turn, each will touch you three times, trying to make you mess yourself. You will try to contain yourself, exhibit your control. You must prove your mettle. Show some spine.' Kurt nodded, excitement twisting with dread, the best of feelings, and listened to the rustle of whispers and clothes being shed. He wondered who was out there, if he had met them before in one of the crowded coffee shops or clubs that Marie had pulled him through, foreign and mute, what they looked like…were they all women, or had Marie included men in this? His jaw clenched, and he fought the urge to buck and twist, to try to pull free and *see*.

Now in his extremity, someone came, and he heard a soft chorus chant out *Un,* then felt the hands. Warm fingers traced a feather touch on his lips, one parting them to stroke gently through and slip along teeth and tongue, then away. They came again and he sucked at them, hot and slim and long-nailed, and he could see in his mind the stain of ash and nicotine that must mark them. *Deux* came the chant, and spider light the fingers traced circles around his nipples before moving in to roll and tug them into hardness. Too light, a tickling torture that tormented as it pleased. *Trois*, and the hands lifted away, were gone, and then settled down again on his cock. Like a startled bird, it jerked up at the touch, and Kurt gasped at the intensity, felt how close he was to coming just with these first caresses. He heard laughter, and his panic and desire tightened as he fought to keep himself from climaxing as a hand wrapped around his shaft, firmly squeezing as another finger stroked the tip of his sex and spread the droplet of slick liquid that clung there over its swollen head. Kurt whined with the pleasure and felt himself move, hips fucking the hand even as he tried to reign himself in. Then the touch was gone, and he was alone and trembling on the floor.

'Don't embarrass me, pet. At least try to pretend you're not pathetic.' Marie's voice was still light, but there was the cold note of threat to it that Kurt knew well, a promise of punishment if he were to disappoint. Listening to her, he didn't notice the approach of the next person until the word *Un* cut through the air and he felt lips touch his ears, teeth bite light on the lobe. The sudden touch was more startling than erotic. He managed to regain some control even as he yelped at the contact. With *Deux* the mouth lifted and touched his throat, sucking and biting him lightly over the lines of his pulse, a sensation that always went through him. His newly found control began to slip rapidly as teeth pressed into his skin, until he felt something new, a harsh scrub against his neck that made his hands clench even before the word *stubble* could form itself in his head. A new twisting anxiousness brought with it another wave of lust, and he began to really feel it now, the dizzy pull of separation that came over him during an intense session of dominance, when he really lost himself in what was happening and let go of everything but the experience. He missed the word *Trois* entirely, only knew distantly that it must have been spoken when he realized that the mouth was gone from his neck, that instead it had taken the tight knot of his balls into its warmth. Pulling free, he floated in the sensation of the tongue that twined and lapped at him until it was gone.

Distant soft laughter, scolding French as bodies shuffled, a murmured *Un,* then hard soft against his lips a nipple pressed, while the other breast's heat brushed against the side of his face. He opened his mouth and let it in to suckle, nursed on sweat and nicotine until it was lifted away. He licked his lips after it had slipped from them, missing the comforting erotic touch of it in his mouth, then came the next count. With *Deux* he felt both breasts return, large and heavy, not Marie's. They pressed against his chest, big nipples rubbing over his small ones, their heavy softness stroking across him, the silk of them burning trails across his skin. *Trois*, and down his chest

136

and belly they stroked, finally brushing over his cock so that he was cradled in the space between. She moved, pressed her breasts together; Kurt felt himself wrapped in them, surrounded by their softness until she slowly pulled away. Kurt lowered his hips, slowly realizing he had raised them to thrust deeper into the cleavage whose heat still ghosted on his skin. Outside of his head, out there, he heard more talking, the clink of glasses, and twisting anticipation and shame moved in slowly quickening currents through him.

Footsteps finally close again, and a whispered *Un* followed by heat and scent and suffocation as a cunt pressed against his mouth. His gasp flooded his mouth with the taste of her, and he lapped at the soft flesh, not caring that he could only barely breathe. The woman pushed herself down into his face as he pressed his tongue up into her, and he heard a distant moan muffled by her thighs and felt her legs tremble against him. With a reluctant seeming slowness she moved then, pulling her sex away from his hungry mouth and went sliding down him until he felt the hot wetness of her resting on the skin of his chest. Lost, Kurt licked her taste from his lips and waited for what would come next. With *Deux,* her small, sweat slicked hand grasped his cock and pulled it up, and he groaned through clenched teeth as his body arched, working desperately to help her sheathe the painful hardness of his cock in her. Warm wet lips brushed him, then with one strong motion she rose up and then came down on him, her cunt clenching his cock as tightly as her hand had. In his distant space, Kurt could feel the currents of desire and torment begin to spin in him, to strengthen and turn in a growing gyre, a storm of release in whose slowly shrinking eye he centred himself. Another moan from the woman who rode him echoed through the eye,

137

and from some far place he heard Marie say something in a different language. The woman above him stopped her rocking, relaxed her body's grip on him and stood, leaving him wet and groaning in the storm. He could hear Marie's soft laughter somewhere above him, and he knew she knew where he was.

In a soft mutter he heard another order from her, then *Trois,* and the woman returned, pressing down on him again, naked skin warm against his chest, hair brushing across his face, buttocks pressed against his hips. The tip of his cock brushed against the hollow sheltered between her soft cheeks and he pushed forward as she pushed down, helping him sink onto her. He thrust hard, groaning, straining against the ropes that held him as the eye of his storm began to fray and collapse, all control lost as he fought to reach out to hold whoever it was down on him so he could finish; sheathed in her flesh, and with a sudden desperate cry, he was slammed back into himself, sensation pouring through him as he shuddered and came in her.

When he finally stilled, his body slowly relaxing back to the floor below him, he could feel that the woman above him still moved and thrashed, her hands gripping tight on his forearms and her feet hooked around his calves. He pulled in his breath and listened to her whimpers, began to wonder about them as his heart stopped pounding, then someone yanked the blindfold away from his eyes.

On him, a woman, slim and small with short dark hair panted, thrusting her hips up to Marie who stood over her and rubbed her stocking clad foot over the woman's cunt. Marie flicked ash from her cigarette and stared down at Kurt, then flicked her eyes to the woman that he was buried in as she shuddered, groaned and stilled. Kurt felt her ass pulse around him as she came, and a low wash of pleasure went through him, making him close his eyes and sigh.

'Not so long then, my pet. Your control is lacking.' Kurt opened his eyes and stared up at his mistress, unable to cope with answering her. Behind her a couple stood, a heavy woman bare to the waist and a slim man with a thin graze of stubble. They spoke to each other in French, then the woman said something to Marie. She looked at the two of them, her foot still pressing down on them both, and then she nodded. The couple smiled, and without another word gathered up the woman's shirt and bra and disappeared out the door.

When the sound of the apartment's door clicking shut came, Marie lifted her foot away, dropped the smouldering butt of her cigarette into a half empty glass of wine, and then plucked a short length of chain from around her wrist and snapped one end to the collar around Kurt's neck, the other to the woman's identical collar.

'She is Gretchen. She belongs to me now, like you. A German, and another fucking purist non-smoker. You should get along fine.' Marie stepped back and stared down at them. 'Another thing in common, she doesn't speak French either. Or English. Bonne nuit, my pets.' Marie turned and stepped out of the room, snapping off the light and closing the door, leaving Kurt and Gretchen bound together by flesh and chain on the floor in the smoke and shadows.

A Master And A Slave
by Mark Steinhardt

When I was in my mid teens I felt a sudden urge to do some reading and give myself an education. For want of a personal guide, I took the advice of the wise people at Penguin. If the book had a black spine (classics) or a grey spine (modern classics) then it must at least be worthy of my consideration. Orange spines were risky. They might be second-rate, frivolous even, and I wanted *serious* reading.

After Kafka, Flaubert and Plato I felt obliged to wade into the Russians. I don't think I ever finished one and after all these years I only remember how long it took carriages to get our aristocratic hero from the gates of his estate to the front door of the house. But I do remember reading an introductory essay on Ivan Turgenev that told me that at fifteen (my age) a kitchen maid was sent by his mother to his room to initiate him in the ways of love. I found this a transfixing thought. I was profoundly envious back then; now I am merely delighted by the imaginative possibilities, and no amount of hard-headed knowledge about the plight of the Russian poor and the abuse of power can spoil it.

As Turgenev remembered it decades later, the girl came up behind him and took handfuls of his hair and said 'Come.' That's all. Now, the future novelist was a tall lad, later to run to fat and be known as the 'gentle barbarian', so we may suppose he was seated, reading a slim volume of poetry, soft-bound in chamois leather, perhaps in the conservatory after dinner before the long summer twilight. He was engrossed in the romantic visions of Pushkin and did not hear Anna slip into the room.

She pulls back his head by his clean, black hair and they look at each other upside down. He must be very confused. He has noticed Anna and been disturbed by her but she has never touched him and no one, least of all a servant, has ever stood over him in this way. But he senses something new and closes his book and remains as she has placed him, looking up into her strange inverted eyes, the cane chair creaking and the low reddening light blushing her throat. A coil of blond hair escapes from her cap and bounces gently. Anna holds this moment of reversed roles for as long as she dare, looking into his soft, smooth face, the healthy teeth in the half-opened mouth, then down to the large, clean, unbroken hands on the book.

She speaks her single word. It is enough. He is used to unexplained orders from his mother and supposes that by some roundabout means this is one of them. When the girl lets fall his hair and leaves the room, he follows.

It is 1833 and Anna is a serf. She may be sold, flogged, separated from her family, branded or banished to Siberia. Without permission of her masters she may not leave the estate, rent land, borrow money, earn wages, own property or marry. She has not chosen to work in the kitchen of the great house but she considers herself fortunate. While Ivan's mother is a fearsome, half-mad sadist who beats her children and servants daily for the most trivial offences

141

and often for the pleasure of it, Anna enjoys the constant proximity of food, a clean, dry room and existence on the periphery of gracious living. And better the exhausting heat of the ovens than the annual struggle to endure the interminable Russian winter down in the village.

Anna leads on upstairs, very slowly, trying to glide within her skirts, making a soft rustling sound in the quiet of the evening, bathing as much in the pleasure of being excused her normal duties as in the prospect of her new and special role. Her hand on the balustrade is white from baking, where normally by now it would be red from pot-scrubbing.

It may be an order and she may have no choice, but this is a private matter and she glances along the landing before slipping into Ivan's room and closing the door. Though she has seen it many times when helping the chambermaids, on this occasion it is utterly new. Where she was an outsider, hurrying a task, fearful of displeasing her mistress, now she belongs, is here for a purpose of her own, to share this room, command this room, even if only for a while. She looks at the brass bed with its rich mountain of white linen and smiles. That evil bitch; what can she know of this?

Ivan follows Anna into his room and for him too it is quite changed. What was merely a place of retreat from the capricious tyranny of his mother is now alive with the intensity of...something. He is not sure what. Oh, the mechanics, yes – gentleman or serf, they are all country people – but something more than that and he doesn't want to know, not articulate it, pin it down with words in his usual way. He senses that he should say nothing, think nothing; just experience.

Anna turns to him, steps close and looks up and their eyes meet again, but this time the right way round. They are both startled to bridge so suddenly the chasm of their social distance. She links her hands behind his neck and draws him down. It is her first kiss without revulsion, without holding her breath against the stench of an old man's rotten mouth. For Ivan it is simply his first kiss and the shock unbalances him. He reaches for the cool brass rail of his bed as Anna steps back.

'Undress,' she says, softly, the word stretched and savoured, but unmistakably an order. It thrills her to give it. This once only, she will have the knowledge and the power. She has observed her young master at the miracles of writing and reading, and so comfortable in the alien melodies of French and felt ashamed of her ignorance, but not here and not now.

Ivan struggles out of his boots, still holding on to the bed. He shrugs his jacket to the floor and pushes his braces off his shoulders. He treads down his breeches and stands for a moment before Anna in a long, loose shirt. It is the primitive, collarless, square-cut undergarment everyone wears, and Anna sees before her a youth like those who might be within her reach – were she but given the choice. She smiles and nods to give him the confidence and Ivan takes the neck of the shirt and pulls it over his head.

Anna is the same age as Ivan but had to give up her virginity a year ago. She is betrothed to a man from the village, a widower friend of her father. He has demanded and been granted the right to prove his virility and the girl's fertility before marrying her, so twice a week the old goat opens his breeches and forces her legs apart on a heap of rags on top of the stove in his hut. The encounters are mercifully brief but Anna never feels free from the stench of him or from his ugly, poxy face above her in her dreams. Her father considers the village postman a good catch for his daughter and actively sought permission for the union from Old Turgenev, who himself likes to catch Anna unawares at her duties and grab her breasts to bruising. 'You like a bit of that, don't you, Anna?' he laughs, and she wonders how he could possibly imagine that she would. He gropes under her skirts and there is nothing she can do. If she complains, the Mistress will certainly blame her and she will be beaten and dismissed.

But when this boy before her lifts the shirt up and over his head and drops it to the floor, it is her turn to be unbalanced by the glory of him, standing there, clean and smooth and perfect, and his root standing out in front, tall and strong. That dried-up bitch. She doesn't know how much I want this. Probably thinks it's a punishment. Thinks we're all like her, all skinny and burnt out with rage.

'Go to bed,' she whispers. Before they even touch, the heat in her belly makes sense of the love stories told by her bedfellows as they sit up round the sewing basket in those precious moments before sleep or wash each other's hair in gatherings from the meadows.

Ivan flings back the great bag of goose feathers and throws himself into the centre of the mattress, turning in the air like a fish. Anna glimpses yellow and red marks on his back from old and fresh beatings. How that woman hates beauty. He falls back against the heap of pillows with a soft thud, sleek and dark in the failing light.

Anna lights a candle, closes the curtains and locks the door. Returning to the bed, she says, 'Watch very carefully, and learn.'

Ivan puts his hands behind his head and raises one knee. His root sways heavily and his onions slip plump and shining between his thighs. The horsehair mattress mutters as he settles.

As instructed, Ivan studies each move of Anna's undressing with the greatest care. She is wearing most of what she possesses. There are four skirts in all, each delayed by knotted tapes which must be swung to the front in a whisper of promise. He watches her soft, stubby fingers tease open the tie, fold the cloth and drop it over the bed-rail with a fluttering of the candle. After the fourth, there is only the hem of her shirt to mid-thigh, and Anna observes his root leap and she fears to spoil the moment.

'Be still,' she says, 'don't hold yourself tight.'

Ivan breathes deep and slow as Anna lifts each knee in turn towards his face and reaches to remove a canvas slipper. He peers into the dark between her legs but the fall of the shirt and the position of the candle allow him no more than possibility.

Anna straightens up and looks to the lacing of her tight-fitting bodice. Her bosom swells above it as she inhales. How full I am, like a tree in blossom. In a few years it will have passed, but this is my time and I must have it.

When she draws the lace from its rings, the restraint falls away and her body can relax into its natural shape inside the shirt. Unlike Ivan's, hers is slit to the waist and closed with little bows of red ribbon. The area usually hidden by the bodice is decorated with patterns in coloured thread; the secret creativity of the servant-girls' bed in the attic. No one else has seen it before. It is more private than her body. Almost as private is her hair. She pulls off her cap and the hidden treasure spills to her shoulders, dark gold in the candle-light.

Ivan watches Anna untie each bow in turn and Anna watches in case his cream should burst out and pool in his birth-scar. She knows that she might fall for a child with that cream and knows that she would be sent away and married off quickly – probably to someone lower than the postman. But a serf, particularly a girl, does not live by future hopes, but by whatever she has now. And what she has is right here. With or without orders she would not be elsewhere and is prepared to take her chance.

The last bow is undone and Anna pauses to observe the beautiful lines up the side of the boy's chest and upraised arms, framing his head. Now she draws the shirt up and away and Ivan sees how her breasts bob solidly when she lowers her arms, how her ample flesh folds above her hips, how her belly is as rounded as a drunken puppy's, how her face is as smooth and beautiful as a peach and how she smiles as she raises one knee and places it beside his hip and lifts the other up and over him. She leans forward to kiss him full and deep and Ivan takes a heavy breast in each hand and breathes the camomile in her hair. Anna pulls away from his mouth and sits up and lowers all her weight onto his root, so that it lies between her lilies and she slides on her juice, slowly back and forth.

She cannot wait, and nor can he. She raises herself and takes his root with both hands and guides it to the place. Ivan is holding the folds at her waist as she sinks onto him and she feels him burst into her immediately. She senses some similar explosion in her own body, just out of reach.

'That's just a beginning. There is much more.'

Ivan is unable to reply.

Anna runs her hands over his chest, keeping him inside. He is magnificent, and so is she, and what they have done feels like everything she needs. Ivan's hands on her back find her own recent wounds and she winces. That scrawny bitch. I wish she was watching. I'd love to show her what she's never had. Make her cry.

Anna lifts herself a little and Ivan's root falls wetly and heavily out of her. She slips to the side of him and places her head in the hollow of his shoulder. He begins to explore the sumptuous richness of her, from her hair to her throat to her breasts to…ah yes. Oh yes, how quickly he learns, this boy. She opens herself, arms and legs and mouth, and they roll in the crisp linen and she feels that fire rising again; a little nearer this time. She is full of rude ideas that excite and amaze her. She darts down and gives the end of his root a quick lick. It leaps to readiness and she throws herself back with a laugh which turns to a gasp as he enters her. As she reaches for that burning and feels it coming, coming, she has time to relish her triumph.

I will make him love me and she will send him away to school in the city and he will hate her for the rest of her life.

Later, as the evening cools, they pull up the goose-feather bag and stare into each other's eyes in the last of the candle. They have spoken very little. Language can only divide them. When Ivan falls asleep with his arms around her, Anna peers through half-closed eyes at the candle-stars on the brass rails and comes to a certainty.

She will fight her marriage, she will find herself a young man. She will shame her father and Old Turgenev with her youth and if they take no notice, which is very likely, she will *still* find herself a young man. She cannot live without this pleasure and this beauty. When all the rest of her life will be so hard, she must have this, and later the memory of this, to bear it.

A Trick Of The Light
by Imogen Gray

It's Friday evening and as I load the dishwasher I try not to think how weary I am feeling. Sam has had a busy day too, I've heard about it over dinner, his unreliable office staff and how the majority are taking time off due to 'stress'.

'Stress!' he exclaims, they've never done a day's work in their lives, how can they have stress?'

I turn the dial, it clicks and I hear the whoosh of water beginning to fill the dishwasher. It's a signal to Sam; he will appear in the doorway and wink at me. I know this because it's Friday and for the greater part of our married life we always have had sex on a Friday evening. And there he is, one arm resting on the doorframe, I notice he is looking older than his forty-four years but, as he winks, he smiles and his face lifts, I catch a glimpse of the young man I once knew.

'Time for bed then,' he announces, it is more of a statement than a question.

'Of course.' I say making my way past him towards the stairway. I wish he would take my hand or tap my bum or something but he never has and I think it's too late to ask him to change.

In our bedroom we fall into our pattern of bed preparation, we are like synchronised swimmers in our own home, an intricate pattern of our bodies weaving but not actually touching. Sam is in the en suite, cleaning his teeth, gargling with mouthwash. The laundry bin lid shuts with a bang but I know he'll still be wearing his boxer-shorts, and will remove them just as he gets into bed. I use the family bathroom, and after fourteen years of marriage I still dab a little perfume in my cleavage. My nightdress is short, Sam commented on it once in a disapproving way. The lights are off when I return to the bedroom but it's not completely dark, there is a gap in the curtains and the street lamp outside the window shines orange. As I slide into bed Sam places his hand gently on my thigh, I turn to kiss him, we rarely use tongues, although I can detect his mouthwash, it's spearmint and too strong. We dispense with foreplay, Sam is aroused almost immediately and manoeuvres himself on top of me. As our faces meet he kisses my forehead. I raise my nightdress, shuffling gently so it's above my bottom. He pushes hard to enter me, I've learned over the years how to relax my legs, he groans very quietly. In the semi-darkness I can see his face, eyes closed and brow creased. It will not take long, Sam always comes quickly, a little bead of sweat will appear on his top lip, he will groan and it will be my cue to breathe and gasp. As he comes he shudders and for a moment his body weight falls heavily onto mine. He rolls to one side and instantly grabs at the box of tissues at the side of the bed. Before he slips into a contented sleep he kisses me again, just once on the forehead. It's not so bad, once a week and my man is happy. Tomorrow as he washes the car and mows the lawn he'll wave to me as I stand at the kitchen window. I'll smile and wave back happily for he doesn't know, after three years, he still doesn't know.

Ritchie is twenty-five. When I met him he was the most arrogant and gorgeous man I had ever come across. Three years on not much has changed, he's fiercely independent, a solitary soul who keeps everything about himself and his life guarded. I met him on a rare night out with my girlfriends; we kept colliding into each other visiting the bar. I remember smiling and saying something trite like 'fancy bumping into you again' and he offered up a half smile. By the end of the evening we were both at the bar for last orders and, fuelled by too many white wines, I felt confident enough to attempt to chat to him. He barely acknowledged me; instead he slid his business card across the bar to me, collected his drinks, turned and wandered back to his friends. Most of me wanted to leave it there on the bar, its sharp white crispness soaking up the beer slops, but the temptation and intrigue got the better of me so I grabbed it and closeted it away in my handbag.

It took me two weeks after that night to muster up the courage to ring him. Surprisingly he remembered who I was and commented how long it had taken for me to get in touch. Within minutes he had made arrangements for us to meet at a small pub miles away. And so it started – my meetings with Ritchie. Within weeks we dispensed with pubs, I would visit him at home and three years later I still do.

I have a key; I've been discreet enough to keep it on a separate ring, zipped away in the back of my purse. As I arrive, it's beginning to rain. I like to visit Ritchie in the rain. His apartment is light and airy with skylights. The rain can be deafening at times; it reminds me of being a child on camping holidays in caravans, being safe and cosy inside. He's not at home, he often runs late, owning his business and taking hours out here and there tends to complicate his day. I open the fridge; it is stocked mainly with wine, Ritchie being a take-away/eat out person. There is milk so I fill the kettle; he'll want coffee, good coffee 'none of that instant crap!' As I pour the coffee I hear the front door open, then shut, and him throwing his keys on the small table, they jangle noisily. He arrives in the kitchen, his hair damp from the rain; its messiness suits him.

'Hello.' I say, returning the milk to the fridge. Without a word he picks up his coffee mug, it's one that I have bought for him picturing a boat in Whitstable Harbour. He winces; the coffee is too hot, he returns his mug to the worktop.

'Alright?' he asks, but he turns away before I answer. He removes his jacket and throws it haphazardly on the sofa and walks over to face me. He kisses me, a forceful kiss that pushes me backwards. I reach out to him to steady myself. Instantly he pushes my hand down to feel his groin; he is hard. I like it that within moments of him seeing me he is aroused. I run my hand along the inner seam of his jeans, his kissing becoming deeper and deeper, his tongue encircling mine. I can taste the coffee, at first mildly acrid. I can feel his hands on my shoulders, pushing me downwards. I break the kiss and kneel on the floor before him. Deftly I unbutton his jeans, lowering them with his boxers to the floor, he steps out of them. His penis is so hard and erect. I instantly want to taste it, feel the familiarity of it within my mouth. I take him as far as I can into my mouth, cupping my hand around him too, rhythmically I lick and gently suck. His hands weave through my hair, pulling my head back occasionally so he can watch. I can hear his breath catching in his throat. He pushes my head back more forcefully to stop; as I stand up to face him, he smiles. He has a wonderful grin, cheeky and boyish which is hard to resist. His smile is an indication to move to the bedroom. Within seconds of arriving he is pulling at my clothes, feeling for my breasts. He squeezes my nipples hard making me gasp in pain, he laughs but then takes each breast in turn into his mouth, sucking them gently. I can feel his hand up my skirt; he never allows me to wear trousers, his fingers pushing my knickers to one side and feeling me, entering me, one, two, three fingers. He knows that I can climax this way; he likes the control. He waits until I'm about to cry out and stops abruptly.

'Not yet,' he says pushing me backwards onto the bed. His bed is huge, bespoke. With a wrought iron forged head and baseboard; it dominates the room. Ritchie reaches underneath it and pulls out a small wicker basket and flips open the lid. I know what is inside and the thought of it makes my stomach clench with excitement. Firstly he removes silk scarves, then handcuffs, serious ones, not the pink fluffy ones I see in gift shops.

'I'll use these.' Without hesitation he grips my arm, forcing it backwards towards the headboard, I resist slightly, teasingly. He bends down and bites my shoulder hard. I am conscious there will be a bruise there tomorrow to disguise. He secures one wrist then the other; the snap of the metal locking heightens my excitement. Ritchie positions himself over me; an impish smirk plays on his face, it never fails to frighten me just a little. Using the scarf he loops it around my head blindfolding my eyes. The fabric is sheer so everything is now visually hazy, softened at the edges.

'Kiss me,' I urge and without hesitation he crushes his lips onto mine. He draws away to run his hands down my body, hesitating at my nipples, then my navel, circling each with his tongue. He begins to nibble at my inner thighs. I shiver and pull gently on the cuffs; they reverberate against the iron of the headboard. He senses I'm ready and nudges my legs apart with his knees. He lowers himself into me, gently at first but then he forces deeply. Above his loud breathing, and mine, I'm urging him on. I hear the cuffs clattering noisily, it turns him on even more. He lifts my legs high, forcing into me even harder. I can feel in the smallness of my back the sensation of an orgasm building, tiny nerve endings springing into life. I cry out to him, his timing is perfect as we climax together. Within seconds, he moves off me and instantly releases the cuffs. As he lowers my arms he kisses my wrists gently. His tenderness is in stark contrast to his earlier arrogance, but he doesn't say a word. And neither do I!

Sam, staring at the computer screen, sighs loudly; no amount of manipulating the figures will make the office budget work this month, he thinks wearily.

He was tired; his eyes became unfocused as they glanced over the series of debits on the spreadsheet. It was Friday and already he was running late. As he began to gather his things his secretary appeared.

'I'm off now, have a good weekend, Sam.'

'Thanks, I'll try' he tried to joke.

'I've left all the post in your tray. A courier came.' She gestured towards the wire in-tray precariously balanced on the edge of Sam's paper-strewn desk.

Sam flicked through it quickly, hesitating at the couriered package – it was in a white jiffy bag headed up 'private and confidential'.

'Thanks Sheila, see you on Monday.

Using the silver letter opener he sliced the top off the envelope and reached inside. One DVD disk; unlabelled with no letter accompanying it. Sam reached across and placed it into his computer drive. With a few clicks of the mouse his screen came to life. A bedroom – well lit with a large iron bed and his wife tethered to it. Sam breathed deeply. A small noise outside his office door made him jump: the cleaners were starting their rounds. Sam ejected the DVD, rose from his chair unsteadily and went to the filing cabinet in the corner. Selecting a key, he unlocked it and withdrew a mobile phone. Accessing the address book he selected a number and pressed 'dial'. It rang twice before it was answered.

'Did you get it?'

'Yes, I've just checked the quality.'

'Good. Is the cheque in the post?' Ritchie all but laughed.

'As always,' Sam confirmed seriously.

'Fine then, we've made arrangements for next Wednesday.'

'Good, adjust the lighting maybe. I have a beautiful wife; she's not to be kept in the shadows,' Sam requested before he ended the call.

He was happy. Tonight they would make love and tomorrow, as he carried out all his husbandly chores, he would cheerfully wave to her as she stands at the kitchen window. She will wave back to him and smile because she doesn't know, after three years, she still doesn't know.

Another Round
by Gwen Masters

'What do you remember?'

She shook underneath me, looking up with those crystal eyes. The uncertainty in them warred with sheer whorish need. My hand shot forward, startled her, yanked her hair with one deft jerk. Her mouth fell open. She panted. She *always* panted when I did that.

'I asked you a question.'

She took a breath. Swallowed. Tried to rein it in. My cock jumped in my pants when she licked her lips. I could read her mind, but I wanted her to tell me.

I shook her by the hair, threw her like a rag doll. She yelped. Her nails dug into my thighs until I slapped her hands away. She glared at me.

'Bastard,' she spat out, coiled like a snake under my hand.

It was always like this with her, always the defiance, even while she conveniently forgot that she was paying me good money to make her feel like an utter whore. She pretended to be livid with the injustice. She pretended to hate me. She pretended that she was above me, so high on a pedestal that even if she spat in my direction, the wind would carry it too far to hit me. Pretending like that was fine, if that was what she needed, but I wouldn't put up with it much longer, and she knew it. She could push, but I could push harder.

I yanked her hair again. She gritted her teeth and her eyes sparkled. She was on the verge of playing Little Miss Wounded. Her games were becoming old hat to me by now. I was getting tired of them, but I wasn't tired of the money. More than that, I was getting interested in a very non-sexual sort of way. I knew I could break her. She *wanted* me to break her.

She fucking loved it.

'Tell me what you remember.'

She purred when I pulled her head back all the way. Her throat was long and pale, sweetly tempting. Which side did I leave marks on last time? I didn't remember. I would make sure to leave marks on both sides this time, just to make sure I covered all the bases. I wanted to give her something she had to hide, something she had to explain. Wearing a turtleneck in the dead of summer in Miami? Wonderful.

'I remember when you told me to fuck you up the ass with my finger,' she said. I almost smiled. She scored a point, turning the tables like that, but I would never let her see it.

'Good try,' I said calmly. 'I prefer to recall you whimpering that you belonged to me while I was reaming out *your* ass. You came when I did that. Remember?'

She was trembling again, kneeling on the bed. She looked up at me but would not look at my eyes.

'You wanted to suck it when I was done. Didn't you? If that ain't a dirty whore, I don't know what is.'

The blush on her face was very becoming. It spread down her chest, hardened her nipples at the same time it ignited her ears. Her hand slowly closed and opened on

156

the blanket, kneading it like a cat while she stared straight ahead. Tears filled her eyes.

'You would do anything.'

I unzipped my jeans. My cock sprang out. Her mouth fell open.

'Anything.'

I slapped her face with my dick. She whimpered. She hunkered down, ass up, knees spread, legs trembling, hands on the blanket, twisting.

'Tell me.'

She hesitated. She hadn't yet learned the ropes of what we were doing here. Sometimes I thought she was too strong-willed. She was the kind a man like me will dream about, the kind that has such a deep breaking point that finding it becomes a personal challenge, a matter of pride. Even when she was doing everything she was told, she still had that pride that would not allow her to be humiliated.

Not yet, anyway.

I yanked her hair harder, pulled her up to her knees with it, and this time the tears in her eyes weren't from desire. That was good. That was fine. Right now I might have been turned on, but I didn't like her much at all. It was the usual combination she evoked in me. The venom in my voice wasn't manufactured.

'Am I going to have to tell you again? I will be more than happy to. I would love to use that new cat-o'-nine-tails to punctuate every fucking *syllable*.'

'I will do anything,' she said immediately. There was that edge of defiance again. I let go of her hair so quickly she almost fell off the end of the bed. She scrambled to keep her balance, and I was pleased at the sudden lack of dignity.

I reached for the cat-o'-nine-tails. She opened her mouth to speak, then looked up at me and shut her lips. Her eyes spoke the volumes that she refused to voice.

I stood in front of her. 'Suck,' I demanded, and there it was again, that hesitation. Right before she could touch my cock, I pushed her away. She moaned. I cracked the whip over her buttocks, and she flinched hard, even though I hadn't actually touched her skin. She really was afraid of that thing. I liked to watch the flicker in her eyes whenever I snapped it around her.

'Wondering what you're doing wrong?' I asked her.

She nodded.

'I'll tell you what you're doing wrong. You're a slut. You're a whore. You're a goddamn bitch good for nothing but sucking my cock. Out there with your husband and your job and your nice little place in society you're hot shit, but in here you're good for nothing but being a hole I like to fuck. So you don't get to *think* about things for a while. You don't get to *decide* what you might like to do, little miss high-society bitch. You do as I say, when I say it, and you fucking *thank* me for it. Is that understood?'

She nodded without an instant of hesitation. Good.

'So you're going to suck my dick. You're going to suck like a vacuum powered by the goddamn energizer bunny. Aren't you?'

She nodded again. I brought down the cat-o-nine tails. She yelped in surprise as the leather bit into the pristine cheeks of her round ass.

'Then what the *fuck* are you waiting for?' I yelled.

She opened her mouth and sucked me in. I grabbed her hair and rammed her. She gagged on my cock. She wanted to pull away, I knew she did, but she was more afraid of that cat-o'-nine-tails than she was of a little deep-throating. She went at me with an earnest need to please

158

then, and I watched for a while as she bobbed up and down. Her tongue was just as busy as her lips were. She had no idea of the kind of skills she possessed. That woman could suck me dry in a matter of minutes if I let her.

I closed my eyes and got into it for a little while: just enjoyed the feeling. When I started to feel that familiar tingle in my balls, I pulled her off me and stepped away.

She stayed right where she was, looking up at me with those bright eyes. The defiance was softer, but it was still there.

'Touch yourself,' I ordered.

She reached down between her legs. Her eyes drifted closed. She rocked on her hand. I got behind her and watched what she was doing. Two slim fingers were sliding in and out. She was sometimes touching her clit, but it was mostly all centred inside, on that spot that seemed to make her shudder every time she touched it just right.

One of her ass cheeks had little red marks on it. I touched them lightly and she jerked. She stopped moving. I waited for a moment, then slapped her ass.

'Did I tell you to stop?'

She started playing with herself again, this time with an edge of urgency. I slapped her ass again and watched the red mark form. I slapped it again, laying my hand in the exact same spot. I watched the redness grow even redder. Then I did it again, and again, making a game out of it, trying to hit the same spot every time.

There were moans now, the ones that came from deep down in her throat, a sexy mating call.

I moved to the other cheek. The bitch had a nice ass, wide and rounded. It jiggled just a little with every spank. I varied the slaps on the other cheek, layering them, watching her whole buttock turn a pretty shade of red. Then I picked up the cat-o'-nine-tails and trailed it down her spine.

She arched away from me, then changed her mind and arched up toward me. I brought the whip down lightly on her cheeks, and she jerked as if she had been shot. My spanks had made her skin sensitive. The second crack of the whip across her skin brought a wild cry of surprise from her.

'Don't stop touching yourself,' I ordered, and she increased her pace to near-frantic. She was hot and wet and going beyond protest. Her moans were almost desperate. I watched her for a while, stroking my cock in time with her thrusts.

Her legs tensed. Her neck arched. Her moans turned to cries. She trembled. Right before she could come, I yanked her hand away from her clit.

'No,' she wailed, hardly able to breathe.

'Fuck me,' I said.

She hesitated, unsure of what to do. I knew her well enough to know the anger was welling up, and if I were looking at her face, I would see something close to pure hatred in her eyes. But I would see passion too, and a glimpse of the woman underneath, the one who was close to begging.

I grabbed her hips and pulled her back on me. Her pussy was shockingly wet. I sat back on the bed and let her ride. Her tits sometimes brushed my legs as she bounced on my cock. I ran my fingertips down her spine and watched the fine sheen of sweat break out over her goosebumps. I thought about everything else – baseball, the old standby. The bills I had to pay that month. Her husband and whether he noticed any differences in her.

I waited until she was on the verge of exhaustion, her thighs and her arms trembling, sweat running down her body. I liked watching her try to hold herself up. I knew she would be sore in the morning. Every muscle would protest when she got out of bed. Then she would remember why, and she would feel defiance and a bit of confusion, the kind of thoughts that would lurk in the back of her mind and make her wonder how much longer she could hold on to that insufferable pride. She would hate me a little bit, and that thought made me very happy.

'I don't want you to fuck me like this,' I announced.

She paused immediately.

'Fuck me with your ass.'

She didn't move for a long moment. I knew she had never had anal sex until me, and having it in this position was something she probably needed time to wrap her mind around. I allowed it, moving my hips slowly, gliding my cock in and out of her pussy.

'I don't know how,' she said.

'Yes, you do.'

She thought about it, then took a deep breath and moved forward. My cock was standing at attention. She slowly moved back until my dick was pressed right between those round, red cheeks. I held them and spread them with my hands, opening her up for what I wanted her to do. She was trembling but she wasn't truly hesitating. She was just being careful.

I watched as her little brown rosebud winked at me. I could have taken the time to get her ready like I had the last time, but I wanted her to take me like this. I wanted her to impale herself without any preparation whatsoever. Call it a measuring of trust.

'Fuck me,' I murmured. 'Now.'

She pushed against my dick. I wasn't surprised to feel the resistance. She worked herself over me slowly, until half of my head slid inside. I wasn't a monster but I wasn't small, either. I knew she was uncomfortable. She paused and whimpered. I wanted to grab her hips and force her down, but she had to do this for herself.

'Now,' I barked. The harsh command was like electricity. She jerked and then she pushed down hard. I hadn't really expected her to do it, but she did – just impaled herself on my cock. She swallowed me all the way in. Watching it, and hearing her cry out at the same time, turned my dials all the way from hot to redline.

'Fuck,' I groaned.

She slid up and then right back down. All the way. *All* the fucking way.

I didn't want to come, but I might not have much of a choice. She was grinding hard and bouncing when she wasn't grinding, and my dick was appreciative. I struggled to remember who was fucking whom.

She fucked me hard. She fucked me with the kind of controlled abandon that said she knew exactly what she was doing. That pissed me off enough that I wanted to hurt her, so I didn't make it easy. I rammed her from below, and she squealed. She grabbed my legs and held on, her nails digging in. I thrust harder and harder until she changed her tactic and removed those claws from my calves. Fucking bitch – even now, even with my dick up her ass, she was determined to have things her way.

I started to spank her again. She gasped out loud and tried to move forward, but I held her hips hard with one hand and spanked her with the other. She wiggled. She was either trying to get away or trying to make me come faster, which she thought might be just as good.

I was surprised when she hissed out 'harder'.

Harder? I was spanking her as hard as I could. My hand was burning. My arm was starting to hurt. Her ass cheeks were red as fire, and she was whimpering with every blow, but she still wanted more?

If this was a battle of wills, I was determined to win.

I started alternating hands: alternating sides. I spanked her until my arm burned, until my hand went past the point of being hot and hurting and into the realm of numb from the inside out. She wasn't the only one who was going to be sore in the morning, and the thought of that made me spank her harder. Just who did she think she was?

She finally put her head down on the cover and cried out, a long and loud wail that sounded like nothing I had ever heard from her before.

She came. Getting the spanking of her life, with my dick buried in her ass, she came harder than I had ever felt her come before. Her whole body tensed, then went limp with the pleasure of it. I could almost see the blood humming through her. Her whole body flushed red, as though heat had been poured over her from the shoulders down. It was the sexiest thing I had ever seen.

I gave it up. Thrust up into her once and came. I roared with the power of it, and held her down on me while I was doing it, until there wasn't another drop left in me. She wiggled a bit but I held her steady until my breathing calmed, until I could think coherently again.

'Are you alright?' I asked her. There was a very long silence and lots of deep breaths, as though she was thinking about how to answer.

'You didn't spank me hard enough,' she finally said.

I was stunned. Anger flashed through me. Then it was replaced with the thrill of the challenge. She was definitely a spitfire. How refreshing!

'You little bitch,' I growled. I picked up the cat-o'-nine-tails.

She turned around and looked at me. Her face was flushed. Her hair was tangled and wet with sweat. Her eyes were glassy with exhaustion. Her lips held the slightest smile, the kind of smile that said she loved this game just as much as I did.

Then it was gone as quickly as it had come, replaced by that look of defiance, that set of her jaw, that challenge from her very core: *Go ahead and try to break me, you fucker.*

'Bring it on,' she said.

I definitely had my work cut out for me.

Fighting Irish
by A. Zimmerman

I was in a foul mood.

I wasn't dressed for running errands. In my opinion you don't run errands in black nylons, a long, black, stretchy skirt and an oversized white tunic shirt knotted at hip level. It helped that I wore white tennis shoes, but I still felt overdressed. I also hate skirts, not to mention nylons.

This pair's suspender-style; technically, crotchless. And they're about a size too small. I'm full figured so this causes my legs to bulge over the top edge slightly. It was a detail that didn't matter when we were home or when I wore pants. It became critical walking around in a skirt. Basically my thighs were chafing.

Pearce had selected my wardrobe for the day so most of my mood was directed towards him, which he had noticed. As we stood in the checkout line at the market he crowded me, his torso pressing against my back. He slipped his arms under mine to catch the handle of the cart, pulling it tight against my stomach as he dropped his voice to an intimate level, his Irish brogue putting a dangerous accent on the pronoun.

'I'm knackered, girl, and I'm warning ye – adjust the eejit attitude or I will.'

Leaning back against him to intentionally imply compliance, I lay my head against the crook of his neck. Pearce shifted his stance to support my change in position as I spoke softly.

'Yes, sir.'

'It's a bit late ta be playing nice,' he noted dryly, his voice still pitched for a private conversation. 'And agreeing terribly quick weren't ye now? Are ye doubting I'll adjust things ta my satisfaction?'

'Not at all, at all.'

'Don't be sassing that fake Irish ta me. Answer honest.'

'No doubt.'

'Emmm. Make yerself useful then.'

He tapped the counter as he straightened away, the lilting accent threading through his words making the instruction sound less important than it was. It had repeatedly proved all too easy for me to get lost in the melodic sound of Pearce's words. Pair the musical quality of his voice with the fact that he was filled with your basic never-met-a-stranger Irish blarney charm and it was easy to miss that his laid-back good humour was backed by steel. Most people missed it most of the time, just as they missed that Pearce was dominant in our relationship.

Granted, we didn't wear stereotypical fetish gear. The only fetish item ever seen regularly between us was Pearce's collar around my neck. To those who understood the nuances of domination, the collar was a clear symbol of my submission. But in general it was simply an artistic statement. The narrow, rounded sterling band created a unique necklace that no one realized was bolted in place. To remove it, Pearce would have to use a special wrench.

In the same way we chose not to hide the collar, Pearce and I chose not to completely hide our relationship. If people paid attention it would became apparent he was in charge. The thing was, no one paid attention. We were hidden in plain sight.

As I unloaded the cart Pearce stood hip-shot, emphasizing his pelvis in an utterly distracting way. I wasn't distracted enough to fail to notice when he picked up a tabloid.

'Don't even think about buying that trash.'

'Right, you'll be thinking ta tell me what ta do now, Rach?' he shot back absently, not looking up from a story about a potato possessed by the spirit of a dead celebrity.

'You need to maintain some decent standards. That isn't it.'

Pearce rotated his hip even farther out to the side, throwing himself off balance to bump me as he taunted,'Ye could maintain decent standards by not staring at my crotch, longing fer a ride.'

'Not so loud.'

'Who's listenin'?'

'Everyone in this line,' I snapped.

His casual cheer, which put the engaging light in his sea-green eyes and lent a captivating openness to his features, disappeared. In a deceptively natural move he squared his weight onto both feet. The subtle shift in body language, like so many other things about my complicated Irishman, was one more thing people usually missed about him. When he squared his feet the width of his shoulders he was, in essence, squaring off for a fight. He was also sending a clear signal that I was not to contradict whatever he said next.

He replaced the tabloid in the rack with careful deliberation. Sliding one hand around the nape of my neck, his fingers curled around my collar, pulling it back against my throat. Stepping closer, he thoroughly invaded all of my personal space. His lips grazed my cheek just in

167

front of my ear, giving his command the appearance of a kiss as his words vibrated against my skin.

'Stop yer chat.'

The no-nonsense tone of his nearly inaudible statement made my heart pound and my mouth dry. Our days were filled with conversation fuelled by Pearce's gift for gab. He talked as automatically as he breathed. By stopping me, he was, in effect, cutting off his own conversation. Obviously I had irked him far more than I had intended.

Pearce tilted his head slightly to the left, the black whiskers of his weekend beard dragging against my skin with a shiver-inducing rasp. Brushing his lips over mine, his tongue sought entry into my mouth. The intimate caress tasted of the cinnamon mints he favoured, immediately eliciting erotic memories of other cinnamon encounters, making my heart pound and my knees weak. Pearce lifted his head, running a thumb over my lips, taking in my flush, effortlessly reading my response.

'Och, ye can be so easy, Rachel Anne.'

His comment made me blush even more. It was true, I melted at his touch and we both knew it. Pearce spent the majority of his time guiding my reactions, the past minute being a perfect example. After issuing an order sharp enough to make my heart thump, he poured on the charm so my heart thumped for an entirely different reason, creating two opposing reactions within seconds. He was controlling me and I knew it, but I couldn't resist. I didn't want to.

The foundation of our relationship was the power of control. Anticipating, conditioning, and controlling responses from me was a critical part of our daily life. A very large part of Pearce's interest in having a relationship with me was his ability to have control. In order to sustain an intimate relationship he had to have authority not only in general, but also over me. He needed to dominate.

In the same way, a very large part of my interest in having a relationship with Pearce was his ability to be successfully dominant. In order to sustain an intimate relationship I had to have someone else in control. When Pearce fastened the collar around my neck he took ownership not only of the relationship, but of me. I needed to be submissive.

Like yin and yang, Pearce and I were polar opposites creating the whole.

His touch interrupted my thoughts. Carrying the bags in one hand, he used his other hand on the small of my back to guide me to the car. To my surprise, he elected to drive. Having emigrated at twenty-eight, Pearce first drove in Ireland. Eight years later he still complained about driving in America. Five minutes later Pearce's preference for being a passenger was proved wise as I disregarded his order to not talk with a sharp order of my own.

'Look left!'

Pearce slammed on the brakes, his right arm instinctively shooting out to brace me as the car jerked to a stop. A truck blasted past the bumper, making Pearce swear bitterly about focking Yank drivers. He ran a shaking hand through his black hair, pushing it into spikes.

'Ye all right then?'

'I'm fine, honey. Want me to drive?'

'No. Apparently I'm needin' ta practice.'

Carefully looking both ways, he crossed the intersection as I settled back into silence. Tense with concentration, his hands at the traditional 'ten and two' positions on the wheel, it took him a few minutes before he could relax enough to speak.

'Ye've common sense, Rach. Ye use it against me, makin' me crazy. Point being, even when ye know not ta talk ye know when ta.'

He drummed his fingers on the wheel absently, slipping back into the rhythm of driving as he continued talking.

'Originally I wanted – 'em…what do ye call 'em? – Doormat submissive? Someone ta be seen, not heard, do me bidding ta the letter. Before ye it was girl after girl who woulda let me pull in front of that truck because they were under no-chatting orders.'

He half-laughed at himself with a shake of his head.

'I need submission, I don't need ta be hit by a lorry. I need a relationship, not blind obedience.' He hesitated, then admitted, 'Ye've taught me that. And ye've taught me ta enjoy someone strong. I don't want ta change the way we are, Rach, but I need ta temper yer ways. Ye push too hard, or yer tone gets away.'

Pearce subsided, clearly debating what to say next. When he went into lecture mode it meant he was stating a case as he saw it and presenting what he felt was the best solution. There would be no room for rebuttal. My stomach knotted as I waited for him to continue.

'Inna reg'lar relationship,' letting go of the wheel, he put air quotes around the word regular. 'There's no problem, is there then? But, we're only mostly reg'lar. There are rules. First, I'm in charge. Second, ye submit, no questions asked. Thing is, ye bloody well don't keep the rules. Which forces me to correct ye.'

He sighed, the candour of his next words surprising me.

'It's bollocks, Rach, when ye're not ta chat I don't have anyone ta chat ta, it's punishment for me. I hate it.'

Pearce spun the car into a strip mall lot. Parking, he turned the car off and twisted to face me as he continued to speak.

'The whole point of a submissive is giving me pleasure. Not chatting with ye gives me irritation. And it doesn't modify yer behaviour. C'mere, Rachel.'

Unwillingly I met his eyes. Pearce propped his elbow on the back of the seat, his head braced on his hand. With his other hand he reached out, playing with an errant curl of my hair.

'Next time ye smart off too much or push me authority too far,' he tugged the strand of hair in his hand. 'And ye know what I mean by too much, too far – I'm going ta paddle ye,' he tucked the curl behind my ear and cupped his hand along my jaw. 'Consider yerself fairly warned, girl. Ye know I'm enough of a sadist ta pull it off once. Ye push me wrong and ye won't sit for two days. Understand?'

I nodded.

'Say it.'

'I understand.'

'I'm gonna do it until yer behaviour modifies ta me satisfaction. I don't care if I paddle ye six times a day. Understand?'

'Yes, sir.'

'Subject closed, Rach. Although I still don't want ye talking. Out of the car, there are things ta be done.'

After running errands at stores within walking distance, Pearce took me to a small tattoo and body-piercing shop tucked into the corner of the strip mall. Holding the door open, he vaguely waved in the direction of the chairs lining the perimeter of the lobby. Understanding the pleasing power of instant gratification I immediately dropped into one. He spun back, his brow furrowed.

'That was terribly compliant, luv,' he tucked his hands into the front pockets of his jeans, rocking his weight back on his heels. 'What's this, then?'

Careful to maintain my silence, I shrugged, surprised not only that he was questioning that I had followed his directions but that he was doing so in public, using a normal tone of voice.

'Go on,' he amended belatedly.

Following his lead, I answered with the casual respect we rarely used in public.

'Nothing, sir.'

'Em. Is this from the conversation, then?'

Although I had taken the conversation in the car seriously, I knew he wasn't asking me about it. He wanted to know if I trusted him or if I was worried about the level of correction the next time I crossed him. I rolled my eyes, my answer dripping sarcasm.

'Like you scare me.'

He burst into laughter, chucking me under the chin, his brogue flaring thick.

'Och, there's me Rachel Anne. Just checking. Sit tight, luv.'

Slouching in the chair, I watched Pearce have a conversation at the counter until a casual nod summoned me to his side. Dropping his hand to my waist, he guided me to a private room.

'Jump up,' he suggested, patting a padded, semi-reclined gynaecologist's table.

Awkward in the skirt, I obeyed. Pearce claimed a seat on one of several wheeled stools scattered around the room, spinning himself lazily as we waited. Drumming my heels, I wondered what was going on and debated questioning his intent.

Since I had several already, tattooing wasn't out of the question. Pearce knew I had something of a fetish for symbolism. Periodically the topic of permanently putting his ownership mark on me came up, but as far as I knew the concept hadn't gone beyond idle conversation. I certainly hadn't seen him designing a mark. Not that he needed my opinion, but he hadn't solicited it, which was out of character.

'You're waiting me out.'

'Pardon?'

'You, the compulsive talker, haven't said one word, you're trying to goad me into asking why we're here.'

The look he shot me had me amending my statement, correcting my flip, disrespectful tone.

'You're hoping I'll inquire why, sir.'

He grinned impishly.

'So ye'll be wantin' ta know then?'

'No, sir.'

'Stubborn is as stubborn does.'

Before I could think of a snide comment about who, exactly, was being stubborn, the door opened. A man came in, greeting Pearce by name with a friendly handshake.

'Ready?' he inquired, shutting the door.

'Aye.'

Pearce gave his stool a push, rolling over to me in one motion.

'Shift over, Rach. Put yer legs over the short side.'

As I did, the man I didn't know sat on a stool close to the short end of the table. As soon as my legs were swung over completely he unbuckled medical stirrups from the sides of the bench and locked them into place. My mouth went dry. Catching one of my feet in his hands, the man spoke to me for the first time.

'Lean back.'

Before I could react he lifted my foot into the stirrup, throwing me off balance. Before I could voice the scathing words that came to mind, Pearce spoke, sliding dangerously on the stool as he lunged to brace me.

'Careful there, Michael.'

A second later I was laying against the reclined back of the table, both feet in the stirrups, my skirt tenting over my legs.

'I told her to lean back,' Michael grumbled.

'Don't be dumpin' her ta the floor.'

'She always so slow to do what she's told?'

'Don't be a wanker. She moves at my speed, not yers.'

'And it has nothing to do with the discipline problems you have with her.'

'There's that, too,' Pearce agreed. 'Especially taday.'

'Why today?'

'It's been a bastardly morning.'

'Why?' Michael asked idly, busy doing something out of my sight. Pearce leaned an elbow next to my hip, his back to me as he continued his conversation about me as if I wasn't in the room, ignoring the hole I was attempting to stare into the back of his head.

'Rachel has a corporate job, sometimes her transition back ta me isn't smooth.'

'How long have you had her? Two years?'

'There abouts.'

'Her professional life still affects you? And you're letting her keep that job?'

'I thought about having her quit,' he shrugged. 'Then decided not ta.'

My blood ran cold. Moving in with Pearce meant moving control of my life to him. Even so, I had maintained de facto management of my career. Pearce had the final decisions, but until five seconds ago I had no idea he had considered anything about my professional life.

'I wouldn't put up with it.'

174

Not only was I tired of being excluded from a conversation of which I was the topic, but I was tired of having a stranger judge me poorly. And I was enormously tired of not knowing what was going to happen. Before I could give voice to my mounting questions, Pearce leaned his head against my angled thigh and answered Michael's disapproval with a mild question of his own, his Irish accent rolling heavily.

'Ye don't have ta put up with it, now do ye?'

'Nope, she's your handful, not mine.'

'That she is.'

Listening to Pearce I had an epiphany. The only reason I had the urge to talk was to exert control. But it wasn't my conversation. It didn't matter that I was the topic, none of it concerned me. Pearce was in control and I needed to leave it in his hands. Trying not to draw attention to myself, I tipped my head back and closed my eyes, inhaling deeply, willing myself to relax.

'Pearce, tell me placement.'

Michael pushed the stirrups to the farthest outside point, taking my feet with them, forcing my legs to spread. A second later his hands were on the insides of my knees, pressing them down and out which pushed my thighs achingly wide as he shoved my skirt all the way up.

'Cut these?'

'Aye.'

I froze from the outside in as scissors slashed my panties. I could feel my face flaming at being fully exposed. Instinctively, I wrapped a quivering hand around my collar for support and waited. Gritting my teeth I concentrated on ignoring the touch of unfamiliar fingers between my legs. My heart thundering in my ears blocked all other sound. Eventually a clamp was positioned on an outer lip and screwed down tight.

Terrified, it was all I could do not to react. Pearce knew how negatively I viewed genital piercing. Focusing on the fact that I trusted him, I forced myself to breathe deep and slow, counting to five with each breath. A minute later I relaxed completely, soaring into the warm silence in my head.

The clamp being removed without a piercing happening pulled me back. Pearce pushed my knees together before he lowered my legs. I kept my eyes closed, drifting, letting the warmth of his familiar touch guide me. It wasn't until he started talking that I started to really pay attention.

'Rachel?'

'Yeah.'

'Yeah?' He echoed with a terrible American accent, making me laugh.

'Don't imitate me.'

'Och, don't be so casual.'

'No, sir.'

'Are ye back, Rach?'

'Yes, sir.'

'So what's this then? I was pushing, but enough fer ye ta go inna subspace?'

'I didn't mean to –'

'I know,' he caught my wrists, pulling me to a sitting position. Kissing my brow, he rested his forehead against mine. 'I was focking around. Ye wasn't ta go all soft.'

'You were just fucking around?'

'Don't take that tone,' he warned, framing my face in his hands. 'I'll fock with you when I want, Rachel Anne.'

'Yes, sir,' I agreed without conviction.

Understanding the implication of my tone, his jaw muscle knotted and his hands clenched, his wrists tightening against my chin.

'Ye'll be recalling what I said in the car?'

176

'Yes, Pearce.'

'Don't push.'

'No, sir.'

I held absolutely still as Pearce studied me for a long, silent moment. Finally, in a lightning-quick change of mood, he banked his simmering anger, his hold softened and his tone became gentler.

'That's yer only warning. Now, ye don't melt like that, help me with the how come and why now. Put me in yer head.'

He sank down on the stool, supporting his crossed arms over my knees as I protested, 'Not like this.'

He snapped his fingers and conditioning took over. My eyes locked onto him, my mind and body going still as I refocused on him, the small impersonal room fading away.

'Talk.'

I wasn't allowed to look away, but I couldn't meet his gaze. I slid my attention to his eyebrows. On one hand I hated this sort of intense interest in my thought process. On the other hand, this was exactly why I chose to be submissive. I needed him to know me inside out, I wanted to submit to this kind of stripping away of privacy, to not even have my thoughts be my own. It was unbelievably difficult and unrelentingly intimate.

'I relaxed, sir.'

'Over talking about ye like ye weren't in the room, aye, but body piercing?'

'I didn't know about that.'

'But ye never reacted.'

I wanted to shade the truth, to be less vulnerable.

'It was you,' I declared, meeting his eyes.

There was a second of incomprehension then understanding dawned.

'Say it.'

'Pearce...'

'What's the rule?'

'If I can't say it then I'm not ready for it.'

He cocked an eyebrow, waiting. A long minute later I swallowed and began to speak,

'I decided to relax because you control everything.'

'Define everything.'

'Everything,' I repeated helplessly. 'I love you. I trust you. I agreed to submit to you. So I decided to stop fighting, sir.'

'Just like that?'

I shrugged, giving up and relaxing into the inescapable honesty he demanded.

'It wasn't that easy, but yeah, just like that,' I smiled, a feeling of relief spreading through me as I admitted, 'I'm yours. You own me. And you don't have to look so stunned.'

'Ye do this now?' he protested, burying his head in my lap.

'Honey, I told you: not like this,' I reminded him, my fingers playing in his hair.

His voice was muffled in my skirt as he spoke, 'I didn't realize ye were finally admitting me ownership.'

'You've been taking ownership since the day we met.'

'I know *that*, ye eejit. It's slow because you, luv, fight accepting my control.'

'I know *that*,' I echoed his words. 'But you put up with it and you're everything to me. So I got with your program.'

He kept his head down in my lap for several minutes without speaking. Lifting his head, he stroked the back of his fingers along the line of my jaw.

'Right, so ye've stopped fighting, have ye now? I'll be believing it when I see it, but it's the thought that counts, aye?'

I opened my mouth to protest then thought better of it. Pearce watched me make the decision and laughed at my final conclusion, tapping my nose as he stood.

'Careful, that was a decision based on how yer owner'll react. Ye may want ta ease inta that thinking, not over-tax yerself the first half hour of it.'

'Rude, Pearce.'

'Rude, sir,' he corrected good-naturedly, holding me captive with his assessing gaze. 'Yer mine, eh Rach?'

'Yes, sir.'

He dug a hand into the front pocket of his jeans.

'Hold out yer hand.'

I obeyed, unable to still my trembling fingers. Pearce supported my hand in his, raising it to his mouth to kiss my palm. Lowering my hand he dropped a smooth, round silver charm onto the spot he had kissed. The interlocking engraved letters centred on the charm were his initials. Flipping it over I found three delicate lines of engraving, my name, the word owned, and a series of numbers.

'You planned this,' I accused as I realized the numbers were today's date.

Pearce laughed at me again, the lilt of his accent turning his words to music, 'Of course I did.'

It All Depends On How You See It
by Kitti Bernetti

'Of course men see sex everywhere.'

'That's because there's sex in everything.'

'No way. It's just 'cos you're a man.'

'It's true, it's a primal urge, you can't get away from it.' Joe drained his glass and refilled us both. We were having another one of our Sunday evening pub conversations. They could be about anything: Saddam Hussein; whether God is a woman, but we usually got round to sex at some point.

'That's rubbish. There are some things in life which just aren't sexy.' I tasted the sharp alcohol on my tongue giving myself time to get my argument honed.

'Like?'

'Like things you hate, things you can't stand. Things you find repulsive. They're just not sexy.'

'Ok, give me an example.'

'Work, I hate it. I never ever feel sexy at work. I'm surrounded by grey suits talking money.'

'Right Vanessa, I'll look on that as my first challenge.'

I sort of forgot about the conversation after that. When Joe and I had been at uni we used to sit up till the early hours with these dopey off the wall debates. Now, still mates even though we were tied to work and paying rent on our flats, we were reluctant to grow up. After a bottle of chilled white any old tosh seems worth talking about and our Sunday-night specials had become a sort of end-of-the-week ritual. The next day when the alcoholic haze has worn off you're shot back into the real world with a shudder.

I work in the world's unsexiest building. There isn't a curve or a sensuous line in it. It's all uncompromising angles, strip-lighting and magnolia patterned with dirty fingerprints. I feel like a white mouse in an experiment designed to see how long one sentient being can spend in a box without turning magnolia herself.

At least it was Monday, 5.45 p.m., nearly my time to escape. I shrugged into my jacket and put my handbag on the filing cabinet below the mirror to put on some lippy. As I was poised, gloss in hand I noticed the window cleaner behind me in the mirror. Funny time of day to be turning up, I thought, but then windows can be cleaned any time.

Now normally I don't go for big muscles but I guess that's because I never see them close up. I only see them baby-oiled in those horrid weight-lifter mags that make guys look like they've got mumps of the chest. But these, even from a distance, I could see were not oiled and were delightfully real, gift-wrapped in a white t-shirt. And they were coming this way. He sauntered across the rapidly emptying car park with a ladder under one arm and a cloth draped over his shoulder like a cape slung over a military man. In the other hand he held a bucket slopping with soapy water. And he was looking at me. I kept my back turned 'cos it's easier to stare with your mouth open when you're spying on someone in a mirror.

He came over to my ground floor window and stood with his legs apart, grounding himself. Lifting the ladder aside he leant it out of the way against the wall. I stared mesmerized at the strength in his forearms and the way carrying all that weight made his chest expand. Slowly he tucked the cloth in his belt, pulling his jeans down a couple of inches. I now had a ringside view of the line of blond hairs snaking down from his navel to his crotch, like a road sign indicating a one-way street. For some reason, I'd become all fidgety, moving from one high-heeled foot to another. I closed my mouth and gulped. I was going to miss my train. Did I care? Nooooo way.

I really wanted to turn round, to drink in the full force of him but maybe if I had, it would have broken the spell. I could see well enough as he leant down, dipped his sponge in the bucket, and slapped it against the window. Round and round he rubbed, the soapy water dripping down his upheld arm and soaking those hefty shoulders. As he moved his arm right and left, his hips swayed in time, grinding the zip of his jeans against the window ledge. Through the thin cotton t-shirt, the dripping water revealed cheeky man-nipples. Then the water crept down to the soaking bulge between his legs. It barely hid a cock which looked as if it was ready to burst under the denim. A wet patch spreading down to his thighs and the half-lidded look of his eyes made him look like a man almost ready to come.

I imagined myself, turning around. For a second I could see us both immobile. Then, I pictured one of his eyebrows raising a fraction, his lips quirking into the essence of a smile. In my mind, he issued me with a challenge.

I dreamt I walked over to the window, swung my swivel chair and placed myself in it facing him squarely.

My heart was thumping as I imagined easing my tight navy blue skirt up to my bum till I was sitting on the hem. In my mind's eye I took first one, then the other stockinged foot and hitched it onto the window sill giving him an eyeful of lacy stocking top and thigh.

As if he could read my mind, the real man impatiently ripped open the top button of his jeans and yanked down the zip, liberating a cock which sprang out proudly at right angles to me. Stunned at this blatant display, I dropped my lipstick and turned around. He really was the most delectable piece of manhood to cross my path lately. If he was ready to do the business, I thought I'd give him a bit of a hand. I sat opposite him, parting my lips and putting my middle finger in my mouth, watching his eyes follow me as I eased open the top of my knickers and slid my finger inside my waiting cunny. At the sight of my dampening panties he dipped one hand into the soapy water using its moistness to lubricate his dick. Looking soapy and filthy and clean all at once, I could see him sliding his hand rhythmically up and down. His arm muscles tensed, standing out like a relief map of the Pyrenees as he gained momentum. His jutting hips bucked in time. There are few things more erotic than looking at the concentration on a man's face as he approaches eruption. He closed his eyes, opened his mouth and I smiled with triumph as he pulled frantically while his cock shot hot salty come onto the window in a sputtering fountain jet.

Seeing the thick essence trickle down the window sent my hormones into overdrive and I was just settling down to finish myself off when my mobile rang. It plummeted me into reality as sharply as if the fire alarm had sounded. What the hell was I doing pleasuring myself in front of a total stranger when the guard could come round the corner any minute? Shock made my legs straighten, shooting my roller-coastered chair backwards where I narrowly managed to save myself by grabbing the desk.

'What?' I yelled down the phone, standing on trembling legs.

'Joe here. You sound flustered.' I could tell he was smiling. Then light began to dawn.

'You bastard, you set this up, didn't you?'

Itching with frustration, I looked at my window cleaner zipping up his jeans and running a squeegee down the glass. He wiped away all that lovely come and my plans for the evening with it.

'I think I win round one. You see work can be sexy. Was he any good?'

'Good, he was fucking brilliant. Although his cleaning's crap. He's left the window all streaky.'

'That's 'cos he's a builder. You don't think he got muscles like that nancying about with a sponge do you? He's a good friend. I do all his computer set-ups for him so he owed me a favour.'

'You have got to give me his number.'

'Do you want the mobile or the home one? The home one he shares with his wife and three kids, that is.' Joe laughed, somewhat cruelly I thought, 'that guy is so unavailable.'

My 'window cleaner' at this point waved a cheery farewell, stepped into his white van and disappeared like my fantasies in a puff of smelly exhaust.

I had to admit Joe had proved his point. Sulkily I said, 'you made me miss my train.'

'Sorry sweets. Trains are like men though. There'll be another along later.'

'You still haven't won your bet. Not everywhere is sexy. Work was too easy, it closes and there are places to lurk. I'll bet you can't make a 24-hour supermarket sexy. Those places are hell on earth and there's nowhere to hide from screaming kids and old ladies.'

'Good challenge,' mused Joe. 'I need a couple of days' planning time. Go Wednesday evening and I'll prove my point.'

Of course, I was on tenterhooks till then. I was in danger of admitting Joe had been right. After his escapade at work I was tortured every time I called the photocopier man with thoughts that he might be some hunk about to go down on me in the photocopier room. I cursed Joe for turning me into a sort of sex-obsessed tart.

Tuesday was a nightmare. I couldn't wait to get off the train and dash into my local Tesco, and that's a first! As I wandered round looking at the zombie-like shoppers I found myself peering in corners and even surreptitiously pushing doors marked 'no entry' in a feeble attempt to guess what Joe had in store for me. Like Pandora, desperate to open the box, I prowled around unable to leave. I swear I was stalked by a store detective I was acting so suspiciously; I bought a bottle of Chianti to calm my nerves and legged it home.

On Wednesday morning I was so keyed up, I found myself spending far too long in the shower, playing with that nice fine jet of water. I had my eyes closed and my head back when the doorbell went. Hell, all thoughts of window cleaners faded as I tramped, soaking wet and pink from an unfulfilled orgasm to find the postman with a special delivery package. Sitting on the bed, I tore it open to find a walkman with a tape inside and a note from Joe.

'If you listen to this before you get to the supermarket this evening I'll know. All bets are off and I win.' The swine. How was I meant to spend a whole day doing what I was told? I took the walkman to work and could almost feel it burning through my handbag. Every time I sat in a meeting where I wasn't expected to speak I found my mind wandering to that rotten tape. I sat there, feeling the pressure of not being able to satisfy myself mount. At one point I was massaging my neck when unconsciously my hand wandered down, over the light silk blouse I was wearing, to settle over my breast where I found my nipple had hardened like a pebble. When I caught one of the partners eyeing me up as if he could read my thoughts, my cheeks turned puce and I was forced into a mock coughing fit to try and make out I had been nursing a poor ailing chest rather than feeling myself up. One thing you could certainly say of my old friend Joe, he knew how to build up the tension in a girl.

At last I was in the supermarket. As soon as I got through the barrier I plugged in the earpieces and listened. There was a bit of Barry White and then a snatch of Donna Summer. Huh, cheesy. If Joe thought that was going to make this seething palace of consumer greed sexy he was way off the mark. Then came Joe's voice. Deep and sensual, I had never heard him talk like that. Instantly I felt arousal drifting up my thighs and settling somewhere in the pit of my stomach. Joe's voice sounded as if he was lying down and was very, very relaxed.

'Okay Vanessa,' he said, 'I'm in your head now so let's just forget about all those people rushing around. They're in the real world. You and I are going somewhere much sexier than that. First, I want you to grab a basket and start walking upstairs to the underwear section. Obvious I know but it's a great place to start. I've timed this perfectly so we should be exactly in sync, even bearing in mind those ridiculously tight little office skirts and clicky heels you love to wear.' As I walked along hearing his instructions, I listened to my heels and smiled. I never even knew he'd noticed.

'Right, you should be there about now. Look along the rails, to the left, and you will see a perfect coffee-coloured lace two-piece. There's something about skin tone underwear that does it for me. It sort of shows everything and yet it doesn't, don't you think?' I fingered the lace, it was a beautiful set, right at the upper end of their 'finest' range. Joe's voice carried on. 'I'd guess you were a 36D, am I right?' He was. 'Well, this time just get yourself a C cup. This is underwear for playing in and a little tightness restricting those full globes of yours will make for a better game.' My stomach did a flip. I'd always been a bit fed up with my breasts. They were heavy and I had to sort of clinch them to stop them clanging when I ran. 'Full globes' made them sound celebrated. I longed to run my hands over them with pride but, hey, I was surrounded by strangers and I could do without being arrested.

'Now you need some cooling down,' came Joe's breathy tones. He sounded to me like he could do with a bit of cooling down too. 'Go back downstairs, turn right and make for the cold cabinet. Right over in the corner, you'll see the cans of whipped cream. Don't you just love cream? It's sweet and silky and those little nozzles on the can are so useful. Take the can in your hands and just imagine what it would be like to be lying naked on a bed, face down with your eyes closed. I'll bet you've got one hell of a neat arse. I'll bet it's just the sort of arse that cries out to have that little nozzle placed in it and squirted. I can almost hear that cream collecting around your tight little bud, and oozing out of the top of your legs. Sticky, drippy cream, it just calls out for a finger to be dipped into it and rubbed up and down inside those glorious bum cheeks. Can you feel it Vanessa?'

There was five seconds silence where I almost collapsed onto the floor, my arse was quivering like a samba dancer's. There was a guy standing next to me examining butter. Quite frankly, if he'd come up, pushed me over the cabinet and shagged me senseless I'd have got down on both knees and given him a blow job as a prize. I was that horny. I wasn't sure how much of this I could take. I found I was staring at the guy like an idiot. I grabbed a can of cream and darted round the corner, getting some relief by standing next to the cold chicken legs.

'Now, the next stop is aisle 13. Unlucky for some, but not for us.' With extreme difficulty I made my way there and ended up in front of crystallized ginger and icing sugar. The cake making aisle. It was in danger of making me think of my mother. Noooooo!

I stood and concentrated hard on Joe. His voice was faster now, panting. 'Just take a look along the centre of the aisle, and you'll see glace cherries. Gorgeous aren't they? Round and red, glistening cherries. The best thing to do with those little babies is to lay on your back on the bed and have them, one by one, pushed inside you. Boy do those little sweeties pop in easily. Trouble is, once they're there, you need to get them out. The best thing is for someone to kneel down and put their tongue inside that juicy little gash. The first ones almost pop out, the next ones require a good long suck and the last ones need a seriously hard fingering.' With memories of the cream still fresh in my mind, I couldn't take it any longer. I was creaming so hard myself I was worried I might make a puddle on the floor. The swine, he'd won again. I spent a sleepless night masturbating like a woman possessed. But I wasn't going to give up that easily.

I phoned Joe the next morning when I'd recovered a bit. 'It wasn't fair. The sex was more in my head,' and yours, I thought, 'than in the supermarket. You've got to give me one more chance.'

'OK, because we're old friends I give you just one more chance. But I guarantee there isn't a place on this earth you can find that isn't sexy. And if I win this one, fair and square, I claim my prize.'

'If you win this one you'll deserve a prize.'

'Ok my lady, so lay down the challenge. What is it?'

'An old people's home. Now I've got nothing against old people, I'm planning on being an oldie myself one day. But that must be the most unsexy place in the universe. All that boiled cabbage and chamber pots, I can't even bring myself to think about it.'

'Oh, I can,' said Joe with an inflection in his voice which made me think that he was already hatching a plan in that ever-fertile brain. 'Can you do Saturday evening?'

'Saturday evening it is.' I said.

'I'll pick you up at 10.00pm.'

The guy was incorrigible. He'd really got into this challenge thing. I'd never seen him as particularly competitive but here he was, pulling out all the stops, just to make a point. Men, they never cease to amaze me.

The days seemed to drag by as my anticipation mounted. When Saturday came, I was ready two hours before we were to go. This was better than going on a date.

As we sat in the car together I was acutely aware of how close we were to touching every time Joe changed gear. I could feel my knee twitch as his hand came closer, as if our bodies were magnetized. It was madness, he'd almost proved his point, that every situation could be sexually charged. Maybe though, this would be his

Waterloo. In a way it would be a relief because then I could get back to normal. In another way, it would be sad because life would go back to the dull old, same old routine that days used to have.

We drew up at one of those big houses on the outskirts of town that used to be family houses but had been turned into a home for old people. In some places the evening's just beginning at 10.00pm but, here, it was as quiet as a library after closing time.

'This way,' said Joe reaching for my hand and bringing me round the back of the house. In his other hand he held a small bag. It was dark and I clung on to him trying not to lose my footing, but enjoying, for the first time ever, the warmth of his hand.

'People will think we're breaking in.'

'No way,' he whispered, 'we've got an invitation.' He pushed French doors which yielded easily and in the corner sitting in a chair was an old man. He smiled without saying a word. 'This is Gordon,' said Joe, shaking the man's hand. 'He's a friend of my dad's. It's his birthday today, poor old sod. I usually just send him a card but he is eighty today so we sort of agreed he deserved something a little more. He doesn't hear too well, and he can barely walk, but he was a real goer in his time. Nowadays he just likes to watch.'

My ears pricked up. 'Watch what?'

Joe thrust the bag he was holding into my hands. I peered inside. 'Please, put that on.' His voice had become low, it sounded a little like it had on the tape. I hesitated, but only for a second. Standing behind the old man, I said to Joe, 'turn away, don't want either of you peeking.' Inside was a nurses' uniform. I immediately guessed the scenario. Poor old guy, surrounded by nurses and never the chance to get an eyeful. I suddenly warmed to my role as I squeezed into my uniform.

'Now Gordon,' I came to stand in front of him, 'I bet you're a very bad patient, always knocking things on the floor.'

His eyes twinkled as he studied the thin blue material and my mountainous breasts bursting out of the top. Normally I wouldn't have been able to carry this through but after Joe's torment of me over the past week I felt so rampant, I needed to display myself. I deliberately turned around and bent down, keeping my legs straight. I was only too aware that he was getting a view of shapely legs, stockinged with hold-ups that revealed chunky thighs. My thong like a little red bootlace was a joke on such a huge round arse. The old guy gave a gurgle of satisfaction and I heard him say, 'Go on boy, I can't get there but you can.'

To my dismay I felt Joe, my old mate, kneeling on the floor behind me and running his hands up my stockinged thighs. I let out a squeak, but he was remorseless as I felt my clit swell to bursting point. Joe, decent caring chap that he is, moved me around so I could see the old guy get his kicks. Joe buried his face in my arse cheeks and breathed in as if he was savouring fine wine then I saw the old man smile as I felt Joe pull my thong aside and drive his tongue up to suck at my exposed fanny-lips. Still bending down and with a burning throbbing clit poking out, Joe massaged my arse cheeks while he poked his tongue into my hole. Then, darling boy, he moved my legs apart and, while he worked with his tongue on the bud of my arse, he pushed a long sensuous finger into my cunny. I was already dripping wet with juices which he lapped up greedily. Swirling his finger round and round it was too much for me and I came in one shuddering gasp.

Gordon was asleep by the time we left. Joe had done the decent thing, and fucked me from behind over the bed. Having a stranger look on just about drove me senseless.

That was ten years ago. Joe won his bet and got his prize. I never realized he'd fancied me for so long. We're still living together now and I still love him. After all, haven't I just proved he's kind to old people and likes doing the supermarket shop? And with Joe, sex is everywhere, and still mind-blowing. Oh, and Gordon. Poor old Gordon's pushing up the daisies but apparently he died with a smile on his face.

The Closest Thing To Heaven
by Antonia Adams

As Demi moved towards the innocuous black-painted double doors, Patricia's words echoed in her mind.

'Honestly, Dem, it's an experience that's out of this world. It's the closest you can get to heaven without actually having sex. What have you got to lose?'

Nothing, Demi supposed, hesitating outside the doors. Nothing whatsoever. She could certainly do with some heaven in her life, particularly of the erotic variety. But now she was actually here, her courage was failing her. She hadn't taken her clothes off in front of a man for a very long time – particularly not a strange man. Even if he did look, as Patricia put it, like something out of the Arabian Nights.

Her fingers closed around the leaflet in her bag. She didn't need to read it – she knew it off by heart.

Treat yourself to an afternoon of pure pleasure. Step beyond the threshold of desire. Satisfaction guaranteed.

Hardly original, but Patricia had told her the experience had exceeded her wildest expectations. And Patricia could get pretty wild.

What if I don't like it, she thought, pressing the doorbell in the same heartbeat?

She could always change her mind. Stepping over the threshold didn't commit her to anything. Not this threshold anyway. She shivered with delicious anticipation. Patricia had told her about the other threshold with a wicked gleam in her eyes.

A man, who looked nothing like an Arabian knight, let her in, consulted his appointment book and gave her a slightly unnerving smile, as he slipped her credit card through his machine.

'Go through, Miss Hargreaves. You are expected.'

She found herself in a room exactly as Patricia had described. Opulent – the walls were draped with rich gold silk and the room was scented with lilies, which were on a small table close to the door. She'd always associated lilies with funerals, but then, weren't orgasms sometimes described as 'the small death'?

A red carpet, which felt thick beneath her feet, led towards another door, which had a small plaque in its centre. Demi bent to read it.

Once you pass through this door, there is no turning back. Only those in search of the ultimate sensual experience should step over the threshold.

Feeling slightly reassured, because sensual didn't sound as scary as sexual, Demi opened the door and stepped inside. This room was smaller and taken up mainly by a changing cubicle, similar to the ones in expensive boutiques. The door clicked shut behind her and a man's voice filled the room.

'Welcome, Miss Hargreaves. You will find a robe and undergarments in the drawer to your right. Please put them on and, when you are ready – step through the connecting doors ahead of you.'

194

The man's voice was rich and deep with a hint of the exotic. Demi wondered if he was the Arabian knight.

With trembling fingers she opened the drawer. Underwear was such a functional term and didn't do justice to the exquisite black lace bra and thong. They were both in her size, which she'd been asked for when she'd made her appointment, and were obviously brand new – their labels still attached.

A pair of scissors, presumably for removing the labels, lay alongside. Feeling suddenly shy, and knowing it was far too late for shyness, Demi took off her clothes and hung them on hangers, also provided. A full-length mirror in the cubicle reflected her image back at her.

She'd prepared for her visit by going to the gym three times a week for the last few months, and she'd had an all-over-tanning session yesterday. She was pleased she'd made the effort. The lace bra moulded over her breasts and left little to the imagination. The thong left even less. Her black hair tumbling over her shoulders made her look wanton. Oh my God, was she really going to parade in front of a strange man dressed like this?

Remembering the robe, which was black silk, she slipped it on, tied the belt tightly around her slender waist and then, taking a final deep breath, stepped through the connecting doors.

She gasped.

The previous rooms had been opulent, but this one put them in the shade. It was seductively lit and smelt of roses, which were in crystal vases on low glass tables. Cream carpet, so soft it felt like walking on velvet, covered the floor. Heavy scarlet silk throws adorned the walls and, as she gazed, she saw other colours within – threads of gold running through the fabric, which formed into patterns. It took a few moments to see they weren't patterns, but pictures – couples making love, in every conceivable position, their faces serene and bodies beautiful.

At first sight the room appeared empty, but as she stood drinking in the beauty of her surroundings, a man detached himself from the shadows at the far side of the room.

He wore scarlet robes that contrasted perfectly with his shaven head and caramel skin. He did look Arabian, Demi decided with a shiver of excitement. He was very tall, and she could feel the power exuding from him, even from here. He was the most amazing-looking man she'd ever seen. And as these thoughts passed through her mind, he moved towards her, each slow measured step bringing him closer, until there were only inches between them and she could hardly breathe.

He smiled, revealing white teeth and she was reminded of a panther moving in for the kill. His black eyes were unfathomable, but he must be aware of the effect he was having on her. She half expected him to rip off her flimsy robe, but all he did was to hold out his hand.

'Are you ready, Miss Hargreaves, for the ultimate sensual experience?'

She nodded, unable to speak. His fingers closed around hers.

Good God, she was practically having an orgasm on the spot.

What would she do when he did – whatever he was going to do?

Suddenly panicking, because Patricia hadn't told her what he actually did – just that she'd love it – she tried to pull her fingers from his.

'Don't be afraid,' he turned, his eyes questioning. 'You have to trust me, Demi.' He lingered over her name, as if it were something special. 'Do you trust me?'

'I don't know you.' Her voice trembled.

'Then it must be an act of faith – this trust of yours. It will be worth it, I promise you.'

They'd been walking while he spoke and were now standing at the far corner of the room. He turned her around so she had her back to the wall. Then, to her surprise he knelt in front of her, and undid the knot of her robe with his teeth. Rising leisurely, he slipped it from her shoulders so it lay in a silken pool at her feet.

His eyes were mesmerizing and never left her face. She couldn't have moved if she'd wanted to. When he lifted her left arm above her head and she felt the touch of silk at her wrist, she didn't protest. He did the same to her right arm and she realized he'd tied her wrists to silken thongs in the wall. Silken, but very strong, she discovered when she tested them and found them to be immovable.

'Silk is what the spider weaves to make its webs, it is the strongest material on earth,' he murmured in a voice that was strangely elemental. Like the rumbling of a volcano, just before it pours molten lava across the land.

Demi didn't argue with him. She was trapped and she didn't care. There was a strange sort of freedom in being this helpless in front of a beautiful man. In knowing he could do anything to her – anything he liked – and there was nothing she could do to stop him.

This thought barely had time to register when she realized he was kneeling again. 'I will need you to spread apart your legs,' he murmured, and she felt his touch on the inside of her calf, moving downwards, feather light to her ankle.

Wordless, she let him move her ankles into position, until she was tied, legs and arms wide apart, held fast by the silken thongs. At least she wasn't naked, she thought, her heart pumping lust and adrenaline around her body. Although she wouldn't have much cared if she was –

suddenly, she ached for him to see her – all of her. She could feel her nipples straining against the black lace and a delicious ache had started between her legs.

He was standing again. For the first time he let his gaze travel down across her body. He looked at her erect nipples, a half smile on his face.

'I think perhaps – you are still a little overdressed,' he murmured, reaching forward.

He was going to have trouble there, she thought, raising her eyebrows. How could he remove her bra when her hands were tied? But she hadn't noticed it was the kind with clip-on straps, which took a matter of seconds to release and remove from her slender shoulders. As if aware of her thoughts, and with another smile, he brushed the palms of his hands over her nipples, then reached behind her and unfastened the final clip so her breasts were exposed to his gaze.

Demi thought she might die with pleasure, as he traced the outline of her nipples with his thumbs, saying with a faint trace of huskiness, 'I see you are beginning to trust me, after all.'

Once more, he stood back, this time his gaze lowering to the tiny thong that covered what was left of her modesty.

'But you are still a little overdressed. Do you not think?'

Demi closed her eyes. She couldn't believe she was letting him do this. Wanted him to do this. Not that she had a choice. He was right about the strength of her bonds.

His hands were on her hips now, slipping beneath the knotted ribbons – oh my God, knotted ribbons. That's all that protected her from his gaze. And they didn't stay knotted for long. He untied them and slowly, tenderly – removed the last trace of her clothing. A small moan escaped her lips as his fingers traced the outline of what he'd uncovered, caressing her pubic bone, moving downwards to her labia, and then spreading her still further so she was fully exposed to his gaze.

Even though she ground her hips away from him, in a strange mixture of terror and lust, she couldn't get away from his touch. And he wasn't in any hurry. Slip sliding his fingers over her and into her – with infinite gentleness, so she ached for it never to stop.

But just as she was on the point of exploding, he did stop.

'We have the afternoon ahead of us,' he murmured, standing once more and cupping her face with his hands, so she caught her own scent on his fingers. 'I think we have much to do – much to explore.'

And then he left her – spread-eagled, naked and helpless, while he strode away across the room.

The waiting was agonizing. What was he going to do? He could do anything to her. It occurred to her that there might be hidden cameras, her body fully on display for dirty old men all over London to lust over. The thought appalled her, but there was nothing she could do.

He returned, a black velvet bag in his hand, which he set down beside her and unzipped. He removed what looked like a cat-o'-nine-tails – its cords made of silken material.

'No,' she said, frightened for the first time since she'd stepped into the room. 'I'm not into…'

He interrupted her with a swift shake of his head. 'You do not know what you are *into* – until you try it.' And with that he drew the whip lightly across her stomach. She tensed, expecting it to hurt, but it didn't. It was like being flailed with silk – too soft to sting, but hard enough to titillate.

He acknowledged her surprise with a slight nod, and then the flailing began in earnest. He lashed each breast in turn, using the cat hard enough to caress and arouse, but not to hurt, until her nipples were so hard, she thought they might explode.

Then he shifted his attention to her ankles, moving the whip slowly up her legs, across her calves, and up still higher to her inner thighs, until she was squirming in ecstasy. He spent a long time between her legs – he was very gentle here – checking her face from time to time, to make sure he wasn't hurting her. But he must have known he wasn't hurting. Once more, just at the point of orgasm, he stopped what he was doing and she moaned in disappointment.

'It is bringing you lots of pleasure – is it not?'

Demi knew she didn't need to answer. That much must have been obvious to him. He had a very good view of exactly how much pleasure he was bringing her, from where he knelt.

He unzipped the bag, once more, she suspected to draw forth more implements of sweet torture, but all he did was put away the cat-o'-nine-tails, before turning back to her.

'It is time,' he said softly, 'for the finale.'

With these words he reached to untie her bonds and when she was free, he massaged the muscles in her arm and legs, as though he knew about the ache that had grown in them from being tied apart so long.

'You come,' he said, with a wicked grin, so she knew it was a demand she accompany him, not an enquiry as to her level of satisfaction. And even though he was still clad in his robe, Demi didn't bother to get dressed – it would have seemed senseless now.

They crossed the room, but not to the door through which they'd entered. He pressed a button on the wall and the whole panel slid silently backwards to reveal a room done out entirely in white marble. Steps led down to a shallow pool, from which steam rose gently.

Demi glanced at him enquiringly and he smiled again, untied his robe and let it fall with a soft swish to the floor.

He was naked below it – and he was magnificent, just as beautiful as she'd imagined. His chest and arms were lightly muscled and his caramel-coloured skin gleamed with a slight sheen of sweat. She wondered if it was brought on by exertion or lust. Was he happy in his work? As her gaze dropped lower, she saw he was indeed happy in his work. His erection sprung proudly from dense black hair. She couldn't take her eyes off it. She longed to kneel and take it in her mouth. To lay, legs apart for him once more, to feel it filling her, stretching her – and it would certainly do that – despite her overexcited state. Of that there was no doubt.

He watched her face, his delight in her pleasure evident, and she sighed, a little wistfully. The one thing that both the brochure and Patricia had said was that there was categorically no penetration. Full sex was off the agenda. It was a pleasure house, not a brothel. What a pity.

He reached for her hand and together they stepped into the pool, the warmth of the water caressing their skin. It had been treated with something and was scented. She breathed in the steamy air, recognizing jasmine and something else in the mix she couldn't identify.

'Sit down. Enjoy,' he commanded.

There were two marble seats beneath the water, moulded so that they divided her buttocks and her thighs. Once more she was forced to sit with her legs apart.

He sat beside her, pressed a button at his side. The pool was a giant Jacuzzi. Beneath the water, a hundred tiny jets fizzed into action. She gasped, understanding the reason for the legs-apart seating, as a jet of water hit her clitoris.

So he wasn't about to personally finish the job he'd so expertly started – she was half-disappointed. But she could no more have moved away than if she had been still tied. As the water inched her nearer and nearer to orgasm she arched her back, giving herself up to it, lost in sensation, loving it, never wanting it to end.

Her eyes were closed so at first she barely noticed the soft touch on her face. But when she opened them she saw he had shifted position, his expressive eyes watching her, his finger infinitely gentle as he traced the outline of her jaw.

It was a touch of such tenderness, and his expression was so full of longing that in that brief moment of ecstasy she would have given up the whole afternoon of pleasure, everything he'd made her feel – just for one kiss.

But it seemed kissing too – was out of bounds. He held her as she came, sliding his fingers inside her at the moment of orgasm, feeling her clenching and unclenching, riding the waves with her.

If she'd been cynical she'd have thought it was quality control – a check to make sure she had indeed experienced the ultimate in sexual satisfaction. But there was something in his eyes that told her it wasn't quality control. He was revelling in her pleasure, glorying in her release.

'So what did you think? What was it like? Did it exceed your wildest expectations?' Patricia's excited voice trilled in her ear. The phone had been ringing when she'd unlocked her front door.

'It was amazing,' Demi breathed. 'He was amazing. Thank you so much for recommending him.'

'No probs. Did he do the tying up thing? – my God, I thought I would die when he took off my knickers with his teeth.'

'He did indeed.'

'And how about the whipping thing with that silk contraption?'

'That too.'

'And the Jacuzzi? Those water jets are something else, aren't they?'

'Mmm,' Demi purred at the memory. She would never forget the water jets, or what had happened afterwards. Although she had no intention of telling Patricia about that bit, or anyone else come to that. It would be their secret – hers and his.

But she knew now he didn't have to rely on elaborate games to arouse or satisfy. He was the perfect lover. A lover with the body of a God and the mind of the Devil – that is – if you considered sex to be a sin, which she didn't: most certainly not. He had the kiss of an angel, too. She'd been right about that.

Placing her hand over the mouthpiece, she turned towards him.

'More coffee? More of anything?' He winked. He was dressed in jeans and tee-shirt, but looking far from ordinary, he was making coffee in her kitchen.

Demi said one last heartfelt thank-you to Patricia and put the phone down.

It was time for round two. But this time she would be in charge. An evening of pure pleasure with an Arabian knight in the dungeon of her bedroom, where the silken bonds, swiftly transferred to the bedposts, awaited them.

Tonight the cat-o'-nine-tails would have a new master – or rather a new mistress. Demi, the dominatrix – she licked her lips – or if she used the full version of her name – Demetria the dominatrix.

It had a certain ring to it…

The Beginning And The End
by Gwen Masters

One day – it was two years, three months, and two days ago – I found your journal.

I literally stumbled upon it that day while cruising cyberspace. My friend Christy, the one from the spa – you do remember her, right? She always hated you – anyway, she sent me a link to her Live Journal account, and, when I clicked on the link, surprise of surprises, someone was already logged in. You had forgotten to sign off after your last confessional. I hadn't heard of Live Journal until that day, but I was very familiar with it a few hours later. Yes, indeed.

That's how I learned about her, or the many hers, however many there were. I lost count, even with all the code names you had given them, like Reddie (cause it was all natural) and Blondie (because that was all natural, too) and Uprising (because those girls weren't natural at all but they looked pretty damn good anyway).

But there was that one that kept your attention, through that whole year you were keeping the journal and even longer than that, the one that you couldn't shake no matter how many women you took for a ride while you were pining after her. She was short and blonde with a great smile and freckles over the bridge of her nose. She was married with a four-year-old daughter and she would never leave her husband, no matter how many times she fucked around on him, because he made the big bucks and she loved her SUV too much to say goodbye. She drank too much, mostly in private but more with you, and she hated it when you smoked.

I didn't even know you smoked, until I read it there on the journal. I'm not sure which was the biggest shock: the affair you were having, the one-night cheats you were committing (stepping out on a wife *and* a girlfriend, you stud, you), or the fact that you, who would not tolerate cigarette smoke under any circumstances, preferred Marlboro Reds in a box.

You probably don't remember that day. You came home to find me in the kitchen, cooking your favourite dinner of chicken sherry and baby potatoes and asparagus. You dropped your briefcase and wrapped your arms around me from behind, kissed that sweet spot under my ear and told me you loved me. I told you that I loved you too, instead of asking how many times it had happened. I told you to take off that tie and change into your comfortable clothes, instead of telling you that I knew the last year between us had been a lie. I asked you if you would mind uncorking the wine and you went at the job like a puppy eager to please, while I was proud of myself for never once hitting you on the side of the head with the cast iron skillet.

Maybe I kept my mouth shut because I had already decided what I was going to do. I look back on it all now and I think maybe I knew, as soon as you described the way she moaned the first time you slid your hand between her thighs there underneath the bar, the way you didn't care much who saw. I think I decided then to keep my mouth shut.

That night I faked it. Twice. If you noticed, you never said.

I tortured myself with that journal for a week. During that time I pulled out the calendar and studied the times you were with her, saw that they coincided with business trips, and determined that she didn't live close to us, but about two hours away.

Then you went on another business trip, and I went to the bar.

It's interesting to sit in a bar after so many years of wedded bliss. I immediately recognized it for what it was: a meat market. I was a woman in a low-cut dress, a display on a high bar stool, while men prowled around pool tables and shouted at the band and stared at me over their beer bottles as they got up their courage. I was sized up, then dressed down with their eyes. I became the subject of bets and locker-room talk in the back corner. They counted my beers even more carefully than I did, and when I finished my third, they started lining up.

There was a tan line where my wedding ring had been. Nobody mentioned it, probably because most of them had the same kind of tan line. I wasn't all that worried about the morality of it all, but I did wonder if what's-her-name knew you were married when you slid that hand between her thighs. Was it your left hand? Did you have on your ring? Did she feel it? Did she care?

That night I went to bed with the first of dozens of men. Well, let me correct that. I didn't go to bed with him, not exactly. I wrapped my legs around him against the brick wall behind the bar, his boots braced among the trash and empty liquor bottles, his breath hot on my neck. One hand was in his hair and the other held my beer, which I took

207

sips from while he fucked me. He was bigger than you. I liked that secret knowledge, that no matter where or how you were fucking what's-her-name, I was getting the bigger and probably better ride.

Sex is better when I'm drinking.

With you it is always good. You're a good lover, attentive and slow until I get mine, then you go about getting yours in such a way that usually makes me come again, even when I think maybe I can't. But when I'm drinking, I do things I never would do otherwise. I go down on a man without needing anything in return. I touch myself and let him watch. I've been with two women at once, and more men than that. I sometimes take them up the ass, but only if I've been hitting the Jack, not the Bud Light. I have to be really sloshed to let some stranger slide his dick up my back door.

I always go very far away from home. I usually drive for an hour or more. I usually give the wrong name to anyone who bothers to ask what they should call me. I hide things very well – I learned that from you. I get my fuck and then I walk away. I get my revenge and they get their rocks off. It works out well, this mutually-beneficial relationship played out under neon lights.

I don't make them use condoms. Does that frighten you? It should. It frightens me too, but I like the feeling of their cream too much to be bothered by it. I especially like the nights I get home a bit before you do, and though I have showered to get rid of the smell of cigarettes and beer and sweat, when you decide you want me that night I like to think there is still a bit of some stranger left inside me, caressing your dick as you thrust inside. The thought fills me with a sweet vindication. Those are the nights I sleep the best, because I know my secret is much darker than whatever yours might be.

But my darkest secret of all is a man named Craig.

I met him at the bar about three months after I found your journal. He was standing in the corner watching everyone else play darts. He sipped from a longneck and drew on a cigarette. He was dressed in jeans and a black leather jacket and sunglasses, even in the darkness of the corner table. His eyes were hidden from me but his hands were not, and when he beckoned me with a simple sweep of two fingers, I should have been offended at the arrogance of it, at the way he wore that air of superiority, as if I was nothing but a dog he expected to come to heel.

By the end of that night I was howling at the moon while he fucked me like a bitch in heat, from behind, while he pulled not-so-gently on the collar he had slipped around my neck. It has always been the same between us as it was from the beginning: hard, unrelenting, sometimes painful but always exciting.

Craig was the only man I ever brought home with me, the only man who ever laid eyes on our marriage bed. That night you were gone on a four-day trip, and I knew from your journal entries that only two days would be spent on business. The other two days would be spent on top of that woman. So I spent two days of my own, tied to the bed while Craig did exciting and arrogant and sometimes unspeakable things to my body and my mind.

I was punished for what I did. Does it excite you to know that? Craig's first order of business was to punish me for taking him into your bed. He told me that it made me a whore. It made me no better than the woman you were fucking, and that was just fine with me, as long as he treated me like a whore instead of just calling me one.

That was the night everything changed.

I remember it so clearly. Every day I think of it, every night, sometimes even while I fuck you in that bed, and especially when you get as rough as you ever get and I clench the headboard, right in the places where I was tied to it for two days.

Craig had warned me. He made it clear that when I brought him into that room, I would become his in ways that I hadn't yet imagined and for ever after, would hardly believe. He was gentle at first, whispering in my ear about what a good little slut I was, about how good my pussy felt around his cock, about how beautiful I was, tied up there like that, my breasts heaving and my cunt already wet enough for anything he might want to do to it.

'These two days, you are mine,' he said.

'Yes,' I told him.

'You will not have a safe word,' he said, and that was the moment I could have changed things. That was the moment I could have said no, when I could have bent the rules, and Craig would have let me do it. He would have honoured all my wishes. But I looked at him and all I could see was you, the things you were doing with that woman, the horrid video of pain that ran through my mind more times than I care to think about, and I knew that I needed to do things you would never do. I needed to have secret knowledge of one-upmanship.

So I looked into Craig's dark eyes and told him to gag me.

He explained to me what that meant.

'I want to hear you say that you understand,' he said. 'I want you to know what this means. It means whatever I want to do, I will do. You won't have any protection against me. You won't have any way to stop me. You won't have a second chance. You cannot change your mind. Do you understand what you are doing? That you are giving me every permission?'

I understood. I wanted what he was offering. I wanted to be nothing but a sex toy for his use. It was fitting that it happen in your bed, where I would have my own secret to hold onto while I tried not to think about yours.

I knew it was dangerous.

I *needed* it to be dangerous.

He made me say out loud what I knew was true. I would not be able to tell him to stop. He could do anything to me, anything at all. He could use me in ways that were humiliating, painful, or even downright frightening. He would not heed my moans or my cries.

The gag felt like freedom.

That night he stalked around the bed with the cat-o'-nine-tails, the whip, the riding crop and the paddle. He pulled out every toy I had and made sure they entered every hole. Then he moved to things other than toys. He raided the refrigerator and found fruit, cucumbers, whipped cream. He found clothespins. Then he went into the medicine cabinet, and the things he found there are things I will never tell anyone about, but trust me, dear husband – it was both worse and better than anything you have ever done to me, and I hold on to that during those times when I think I cannot handle one more night with the weight of the secrets between us.

I still read your journal, you know. I know your affair is over now. I know something happened, but you don't know what. Perhaps her husband found out. She was torn for a while, and she finally made the decision to walk away from you. You wrote about it with a poetic kind of loss that made me sick to my stomach.

She will be with someone else soon, of course. What cuts deepest is that she was the one who had to walk away. You weren't willing to do that, but she was. And why?

She wasn't in love with you.

Now I'm not in love with you, either.

I realized that I wasn't in love with you the night Craig looked at me and for the first time, his dominance looked like submissiveness, when he asked me if I would leave you for him. I told him I would. But there was something I had to do first. Something I had to give you.

In the package with this letter is a videotape. It has hours and hours of sexual romps on it. They all feature Craig. In some of them he is with me, your wife, fucking me with utter abandon. In the rest of them, Craig is with that woman you loved, *his* wife, and he's fucking her while she tells him that he is so much better in bed than any of her lovers – including you.

Enjoy, sweetheart.

Also available from Xcite Books
www.xcitebooks.com

Publication 14th February 2007

Sex & Seduction	**1905170785**	**price £7.99**
Sex & Satisfaction	**1905170777**	**price £7.99**
Sex & Submission	**1905170793**	**price £7.99**

Publication 14th May 2007

5 Minute Fantasies 1	**1905170610**	**price £7.99**
5 Minute Fantasies 2	**190517070X**	**price £7.99**
5 Minute Fantasies 3	**1905170718**	**price £7.99**

Publication 13th August 2007

Whip Me	**1905170920**	**price £7.99**
Spank Me	**1905170939**	**price £7.99**
Tie Me Up	**1905170947**	**price £7.99**

Publication 12th November 2007

Ultimate Sins	**1905170599**	**price £7.99**
Ultimate Sex	**1905170955**	**price £7.99**
Ultimate Submission	**1905170963**	**price £7.99**

Whip Me	1905170920	price £7.99
Spank Me	1905170939	price £7.99
Tie Me Up	1905170947	price £7.99

Sex & Seduction	1905170785	price £7.99
Sex & Satisfaction	1905170777	price £7.99
Sex & Submission	1905170793	price £7.99

 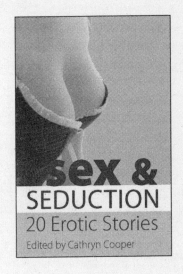